SWEET
DECEIT

SWEET DECEIT
A PRIVILEGE NOVEL

BY

KATE BRIAN

SIMON & SCHUSTER BFYR

New York   London   Toronto   Sydney

An imprint of Simon & Schuster Children's Publishing Division
1230 Avenue of the Americas, New York, New York 10020

For information about special discounts for bulk purchases, please contact Simon
& Schuster Special Sales at 1-866-506-1949
or business@simonandschuster.com.
The Simon & Schuster Speakers Bureau can bring authors to your live event. For
more information or to book an event, contact the
Simon & Schuster Speakers Bureau at 1-866-248-3049 or visit
our website at www.simonspeakers.com.

Produced by Alloy Entertainment
151 West 26th Street, New York, NY 10001

Book design by Andrea C. Uva
The text of this book was set in Adobe Garamond.
Manufactured in the United States of America
2 4 6 8 10 9 7 5 3 1
Library of Congress Control Number 2010924179
ISBN 978-1-4169-6762-0
ISBN 978-1-4169-8549-5 (eBook)

FIRST
EDITION

To all the Facebook and Twitter friends who've voiced their firm opinions on what Ariana should do next, thanks for all your tremendous support. This one's for you!

A PROMISE

"To know Brigit was to love Brigit," Lexa Greene said, lifting her chin. Tears shone in her green eyes. Hundreds of candles adorned the marble stairs of the Atherton-Pryce Hall chapel, flickering in the cool autumn breeze. The black-clad crowd of students, faculty, and parents huddled even closer together against the cold—and their own sadness.

Ariana Osgood held a white candle in front of her, the flame blurring before her tired, tear-stung eyes. Her heart felt like it was collapsing in on itself over and over again, radiating misery and pain throughout her body. She'd arrived at Atherton-Pryce Hall just over a month ago, and she hadn't imagined that she'd become true friends with anyone as fast as she had with Brigit Rhygsted—or that it could hurt so badly to lose her. It had been a week since Brigit had died, and Ariana still couldn't believe she was gone. A vivid image flashed through Ariana's mind. She saw Brigit's body, so slight, so broken, crumpled at the foot of that regal staircase where she'd met her end. The pain in Ariana's heart squeezed ever tighter and her throat closed up. If only she'd been there. If only there was something she could have done.

"She was all about adventure and laughter, and she exuded pure joy," Lexa continued.

Ariana heard a loud sniffle to her left. Kaitlynn Nottingham was weeping, holding her trembling fingers over her lips as if to keep from sobbing out loud. Ariana's free hand curled into a fist, and in her mind's eye she saw herself punching Kaitlynn in the face. Imagined the satisfying crack of her nose and the thud as the girl hit the ground.

Kaitlynn had killed Brigit. Shoved her down the huge marble staircase at the Norwegian Embassy for no better reason than her desire to be accepted into Stone and Grave—the secret society for which all three of them had been tapped. And now she had the gall to stand there and cry?

Hovering next to Kaitlynn was Adam Lazerri, his curly brown hair frizzy and his chin spotty with stubble. He stared at the ground, swallowing repeatedly, clearly trying not to cry. He at least had a right to be sad. He and Brigit had just started dating. Along with Adam was Landon Jacobs. The pop star's long bangs grazed the top of his dark sunglasses as he stared straight ahead. Next to him, Maria Stanzini let out a sob, and Ariana saw Landon reach out to squeeze her hand. Maria pressed her face into Landon's shoulder, looking for all the world like a girl who was leaning on her friend for support. Only

Ariana knew that the two of them were secretly dating. At least her friend was able to take comfort from the boy she loved and not worry that anyone would read anything into it. For once, Landon was not the center of attention.

Ariana's own secret love, Palmer Liriano, stood at the edge of the group, his hands folded at waist level, his dark hair slicked back from his face. Every now and then he would sniffle and blink, holding back tears. Ariana wished she could go to him, comfort him, be comforted. But now was not the time to be selfish.

"If you would all bow your heads for a moment of silence in honor of our friend," Lexa was saying.

Soomie Ahn reached out and took Ariana's hand. The coil in Ariana's heart loosened, and she took a long, deep breath. She looked up at the large photo of Brigit propped up on the black velvet–covered table next to Lexa. It was surrounded by small pumpkins, brightly colored leaves, and mums in gorgeous gold and white. In the photo, Brigit beamed on a white-sand beach, her blond curls lit by the sun. She looked alive, happy, and completely oblivious to the fact that her life would be cut short by a psychopath masquerading as a friend.

For a long moment, everything was still. The breeze whistled through the bell tower atop the chapel, and a boat's horn sounded from down on the Potomac River below campus.

"Thank you," Lexa said finally.

Ariana opened her eyes. Lifted her head. Forced herself to breathe the crisp autumn air.

"I know that many of you have brought flowers for Brigit. If you'd

like to come up one by one, you can take a moment and leave them
here by her picture," Lexa said.

Conrad Royce, Lexa's boyfriend, slipped quickly from the crowd
and left a white rose in front of Brigit's picture, before engulfing Lexa
in a hug. Soomie gave Ariana a slight nudge, and they started for the
chapel steps, hand in hand, as the large crowd of mourners broke
and shifted behind them. Maria walked over and held on to Soomie's
arm on the other side, bringing Landon, Adam, and Palmer with her.
Together the six of them climbed the first tier of steps to the landing
where Lexa and Conrad waited.

"We'll miss you every day, Brigit," Lexa said, placing her yellow
sunflower—Brigit's favorite—in front of the photo.

Soomie started to cry in earnest, her silky black hair covering her
face. "I just . . . I can't . . . I can't imagine being here without . . ."

Ariana glanced at Lexa and bit her lip. She removed her own sunflower from the pocket of her coat and looked at Brigit's picture. "We
didn't know each other for very long, Brigit, but you meant more to
me than you could ever know. Thanks for being such a good friend."

She lay down her flower. Then Soomie lifted her head and added her
offering, still sobbing. Ariana held her breath—held in her own tears.
She and her friends all realized that as Brigit's roommate and best friend,
Soomie was taking Brigit's death harder than the rest of them.

Maria rounded her shoulders. Her light brown hair was back in a
bun, and her angular face was makeup-free. "Wherever you are, B, I
hope it's a party worthy of you," she said as she added her red gerbera
daisy to the pile.

As the rest of the large crowd started to form a long, solemn line at the foot of the stairs, the boys lay their flowers down before Brigit's photo. For a long moment, the eight of them stood staring at the picture of their friend. A stiff wind hit from behind, but Ariana didn't shuffle sideways or grip Lexa or Soomie tighter. She couldn't. She felt rooted to the spot. Like if she tried to move her legs, her feet might stay behind.

"Come on, girls. A lot of people are waiting," Lexa said quietly.

She blew out her candle, and Ariana and the others followed her lead. Soomie rested her head against Maria's arm as they descended the steps. When Ariana's foot hit the first stair, her ankle started to buckle and she found herself grabbing for Lexa to keep her balance. Instead, she caught Kaitlynn's arm.

"Ana! Are you okay?" Kaitlynn's green eyes were wide. She had the concerned act down pat, but Ariana could see right through it.

Ariana snatched her hand back. The idea that Brigit's murderer had listened in on their last words to Brigit made her skin crawl.

"I'm fine," Ariana said through her teeth.

Her friends had moved off to the side at the bottom of the stairs, where they watched the procession of mourners approach Brigit's memorial. Ariana walked over to join them and, of course, Kaitlynn followed. As they huddled in a group, a few more familiar faces from their exclusive dorm, Privilege House, approached the altar. April Corrigan, the editor of the literary magazine, was followed by Tahira Al Mahmood and Tahira's boyfriend, Rob Mellon. Then came Allison Rothaus, along with Christian Brooks, one of Palmer's crew teammates, who was whispering with an angular boy with blond hair. Ariana had seen him around the dorm, always with kind of a placid, distant look in his eyes. He wore no coat over his suit, even though the night air held a distinct chill. As Ariana observed him, another breeze kicked up the skirt of her coat, bringing with it the crisp, musky scent of a fire burning in one of the school's ancient stone fireplaces. Maria took a deep breath and tilted her head back, looking up at the stars.

"God, Brigit would have loved this," she said.

Soomie let out a sound that was half sob, half laugh.

"Not her memorial service," Maria said, rolling her eyes and squeezing Soomie tighter. "This night . . . the decorations . . . the weather. She loved this time of year."

"Especially Halloween," Lexa said, pushing her hands into her pockets. "They didn't really do it up in Norway the way we do here. She lived for Halloween parties."

"She'd be so pissed to be missing yours," Maria said to Soomie.

Soomie sucked in a breath and produced a rumpled tissue from the pocket of her black coat. She pressed it under her nose, gathered herself, and shook her hair back.

"Actually, I think I'm gonna cancel it," she said.

"What?" Lexa said automatically.

Soomie's dark eyes flashed. "Well, let's see. (A) Brigit and I were going to dress up together, and every time I think about that it makes me bawl, (B) I can't even wrap my brain around the idea of digging through the decorations, half of which Brigit shopped for with me, and (C) I can't even dress myself right now, let alone decide whether or not we should serve spider eggs this year! So I don't think that I'm really equipped to throw a party."

"I'm sorry, Soomie. I didn't mean . . ." Lexa's eyes brimmed with tears. "It was just a reaction. I . . ."

Lexa trailed off and Ariana looped her arm around Lexa, holding her close. The group fell silent. The guys eyed each other and surreptitiously edged away, leaving the five girls to themselves.

"Um, well . . . I can at least help with the last one, Soomie," Kaitlynn said. "I do *not* think anyone should be serving spider eggs. Ever."

Soomie, Lexa, and Maria exchanged a look, then laughed. Even Ariana smiled.

"They're not actual spider eggs," Maria explained, tucking her dark hair behind her ear. "Just deviled eggs and veggies constructed to look like spiders."

"I don't know, you guys," Soomie said, looking at her battered black flats, worn over dark blue tights.

"We'll hire someone to finish the planning," Maria said. "Seriously, Soom. Brigit would die if you canceled Halloween."

Kaitlynn snorted at Maria's choice of words but quickly turned her laughter into a coughing sob. Ariana's toes curled in her boots.

Control, Ariana. This is not the time.

But when? How? Over the past few weeks Ariana had done everything in her power to try to get rid of Kaitlynn, but Kaitlynn had overpowered her every time. She'd even managed to worm her way into Ariana's group of friends. And that one frustrating fact always remained—if Kaitlynn went down, Ariana would go down too. She was trapped. Her star was tied to Kaitlynn's. One wrong move and they would both be headed back to the Brenda T. Trumbull Correctional Facility for Women.

"Hey, Lexa . . . is that your dad?" Maria said, squinting into the darkness.

Lexa glanced at the chapel stairs. A tall gentleman with salt-and-pepper hair approached Brigit's picture and bowed his head. As he closed his eyes in prayer, a guy in a black trench snapped his picture. A young Asian woman with short black hair and wearing a staid gray suit stood off to the side, surveying the crowd.

"Yep. That's the senator," Lexa said.

The man walked right over to Lexa, the cameraman racing after him. Ariana saw a few people in the crowd take notice, pointing or whispering behind their hands.

"Lexa, honey, I'm so sorry for your loss," the senator said, enveloping Lexa in a tight but somehow formal hug. The camera flashed as a couple dozen shots were taken. Lexa quickly released her father and backed away.

"Thanks, Dad," Lexa said, avoiding eye contact with him. "You know Maria and Soomie. And this is Ana Covington and Lillian Oswald."

"Nice to meet you, Senator," Ariana said, shaking his hand.

"Hello, sir," Kaitlynn said. Neither girl missed a beat at the sound of their assumed names.

"Girls." His expression was grim.

"And this is Keiko Ogaswara. She's the right-hand woman for my family," Lexa said with a warm smile. She didn't acknowledge the photographer.

"Nice to meet you," Keiko said. Then she turned and hugged Lexa. "How are you doing? Is there anything you need?"

Lexa shook her head and hugged the woman tightly. "I'll be all right."

A pair of middle-aged men hovered a few yards off, as if waiting to speak to the senator. Meanwhile, the long line of mourners continued to edge forward, their mingled conversation an ever-present hum.

The senator cleared his throat. "I have to be on a plane to Boston in an hour. But I'll see you when I get back?"

"Of course," Lexa said with a forced smile. "Thanks for coming."

"You know I'm always here for you," he said. Then, after another stiff, awkward hug and a few more flash pops, he was gone. Keiko scurried off after her boss but turned around briefly and touched her fingers to her lips in a good-bye for Lexa. The two men who were lying in wait quickly fell into step with the senator as well.

Maria turned to Lexa, her hands in her pockets. "Since when does your dad crash funerals?"

"Since my parents are living in separate houses and his family-values supporters are freaking out." Lexa rolled her eyes. "He's all about his image right now. Thus the photographer. I'm sure those pictures will be in the *Boston Globe* tomorrow."

"I'm sorry," Kaitlynn said.

Soomie rubbed Lexa's back. "I'm sure Brigit's laughing about it right now—her memorial service being turned into a photo-op."

Lexa sighed sadly, looking down at the green bangle bracelet she wore on her right wrist.

Ariana looked down at her own bracelet—just like Lexa's, but in red. Soomie had one as well, in blue; Maria's was orange; and Kaitlynn—much to Ariana's revulsion—wore a purple one. The colorful set of bracelets had been Brigit's favorite accessory. So when Brigit's maid had come to take her things home, Lexa had asked if it would be all right for her and her friends to have the bracelets to remember her by.

"Life is so insane," Kaitlynn mused, looking down at her bracelet as well. "Just a week ago, Brigit was wearing these . . . alive and well. . . ."

Ariana bit down on her tongue so hard she tasted blood. Kaitlynn took a deep breath and looked around at the group. Her eyes were full of bittersweet nostalgia. Fake. All of it fake.

"I think she'd be happy to know that we're all going to carry a piece of her with us . . . forever."

As the other girls nodded and sighed, Ariana grabbed her forearm and dug her fingers into the sleeve of her coat, trying to breathe.

In, one . . . two . . . three . . .

Out, one . . . two . . . three . . .

In, one . . . two . . . three . . .

Out, one . . . two . . . three . . .

It was the only way she could keep herself from reaching out and strangling Kaitlynn Nottingham right then and there.

All in good time, Ariana, she told herself. *You'll figure out a way. You always do.* She looked up at Brigit's photo one last time and clenched her jaw. *I'm going to make this right, Brigit. I promise. I'm going to do whatever it takes to make this right.*

A TRUE FRIEND

Ariana dressed quickly the following morning, hoping to slip out while Kaitlynn was in the shower. When Ariana's welcome week team had won the three-part competition and earned the right to live in Privilege House, the plushest dorm on campus, she'd gotten a private bathroom to share only with her roommate. Unfortunately, that roommate had turned out to be Kaitlynn. None of the Privilege House boons could cancel out the nightmare of once again living with her worst enemy.

After Lexa's impromptu soiree the night before, Ariana had gone to bed early, only to spend the entire night wide-awake and tense, her heart pounding with ire as she listened to the steady cadence of Kaitlynn's quiet snore in the next bed. That Kaitlynn was allowed to remain alive and well and was sleeping peacefully while Brigit was rotting in the ground somewhere was so abysmally wrong, it was all Ariana could do to keep from jumping the girl and slitting her throat as she slept.

But that, of course, would have been messy.

The water in their private bathroom stopped running. Ariana quickly fastened her pearl earrings into her ears and reached for Brigit's red bangle. She had just slipped it onto her wrist when Kaitlynn emerged from the bathroom, wrapping a towel around her slim body. The very sight of her made Ariana's blood burn.

"Hey," Kaitlynn said, glancing over Ariana's outfit. "Wait up. We can walk over together."

Ariana laughed bitterly. "You can't be serious."

Kaitlynn paused in front of her walk-in closet.

"Kaitlynn, you killed one of my best friends," Ariana said, grabbing her book bag and slinging it over her shoulder. "The fact that I'm even talking to you right now is making me physically ill."

Kaitlynn rubbed a towel over her short blond hair, still wet from the shower. "We were best friends once too, you know."

Ariana paused with her hand on the doorknob. Against her better judgment, she looked at her roommate, and for a split second she saw that old vulnerability in Kaitlynn's wide green eyes—that craving to be accepted and loved, which had sucked Ariana in during their time at the Brenda T.

But then Kaitlynn blinked, clenched her jaw, and turned away.

"Not really," Ariana said, her skin prickling with heat over having almost let her guard down. "You were lying to me the entire time."

Kaitlynn yanked a shirt off a hanger, then went to her dresser for a bra and underwear. "Like you never lied to me."

Ariana released the doorknob and turned toward Kaitlynn. "I didn't," she said, crossing her arms over her chest.

Kaitlynn dressed quickly, her back to Ariana, shaking her head as she buttoned up her white uniform shirt. "Right. So all that stuff about hating your life and being glad you never had to see any of those people again. How I was a better friend than they ever were. All that was true?" she asked, turning to glare at Ariana.

Instantly, Ariana's skin warmed and her eyes stung. Images of her former friends from Easton Academy—Noelle Lange, Kiran Hayes, and Taylor Bell—flitted through her mind. She vividly recalled how her heart used to leap whenever the guards announced that she had a visitor. How she used to stand outside the door to the visiting room while it was being unlocked, nearly giddy with hope, envisioning Noelle sitting at the metal table with her dark sunglasses on, or Kiran perched with a pile of fashion magazines, or Taylor offering a sweet smile. But it was always her lawyer or her father or some reporter hoping for a story. None of the Billings girls had ever come. Their rejection stung, even now.

"Yeah. That's what I thought," Kaitlynn said, stepping into a blue pleated skirt and fastening it around her slim waist. "They couldn't have cared less. But me? I was always there for you."

"You had to be," Ariana replied. "We were stuck in the same room." *Just like we are now,* she added silently. Although back then it had been different. Back then, Ariana had thought that Kaitlynn was sweet, innocent, and wrongfully accused.

"Well, just so you know, it wasn't all lies." Kaitlynn sat down on her bed and jammed her feet into knee-high socks.

"That doesn't change the fact that you used me," Ariana said quietly.

Kaitlynn sighed. "Maybe," she said, standing. "But would you have broken out if I told you the truth? Would either of us be here now?"

Ariana took a deep breath. Kaitlynn never tired of reminding her that she was the one who had led her to Briana Leigh. That without Kaitlynn, Ariana never would have met the girl and never would have had the chance to assume her identity and start a new life. And Ariana, as always, had to admit that it was true.

"But if neither of us were here now, Brigit would still be alive."

She turned, but Kaitlynn stopped her with a hand on her shoulder. "Wait."

Ariana swallowed against a dry throat.

"I know you're pissed off that Brigit isn't here anymore, but I had to do it," Kaitlynn said. "If anyone should understand that, you should. You got rid of Briana Leigh because she was standing in your way. Well, that's all I did. Brigit was in the way of me having the life I want. It was simple math. There were four spots in Stone and Grave and five people to fill them. All I did was help us both out."

Ariana looked into Kaitlynn's eyes, so calm and guileless, and her heart thumped. Because she realized that what Kaitlynn was saying made sense. Kaitlynn's entire life was at stake here. She needed Stone and Grave to survive. And survival was what it was all about.

"Think of it this way . . . you're lucky," Kaitlynn said, withdrawing her hand from Ariana's shoulder and giving a shrug. "It could have just as easily been you."

Ariana blinked, her heart dropping into her toes. A cold icicle of fear drove its way directly into her heart, and her knees started to tremble beneath her.

It could have just as easily been you.

Everyone was expendable to Kaitlynn. Everyone.

Kaitlynn turned away, humming as she slipped her APH blazer on over her white turtleneck. Like nothing out of the ordinary had happened. Like she hadn't just offhandedly threatened Ariana's life.

Taking a deep breath, Ariana steadied herself, quelled the bristles of fear prickling along her spine, and kept the hot tears threatening in her eyes at bay.

"You know what? I can wait a few minutes for you to get ready," she said, placing her bag on the floor.

Kaitlynn's eyes narrowed. "Yeah?"

"Yeah," Ariana said. "Go ahead and get dressed. We'll walk over together."

"Okay." Kaitlynn looked her up and down, surprised, maybe even wary. "I'll be ready in five."

Then she slipped past Ariana into the bathroom and turned on the hair dryer. Ariana gave her weakened knees a rest, dropping down onto her perfectly made bed. She wrapped her fingers around her forearm and squeezed, watching the door of the bathroom and waiting for her roommate, thinking ahead to the mindless chitchat she would make as they crossed the campus together.

After all, it was all about survival. And now Ariana knew exactly what she had to do to stay alive.

THE GAME IS AFOOT

The large, white-washed dining hall was filled with hushed conversation, the sounds of clinking silverware, and the scent of frying bacon. Ariana walked in with Kaitlynn at her side and turned toward her usual table, which she shared with Lexa, Soomie, Maria, Landon, Adam, Conrad, and sometimes Palmer—who would have been a sight for sore eyes right about then.

Lexa looked up, caught Ariana's eye, smiled, and waved her over. Ariana waved back. Hanging out with a real friend like Lexa right now would be a relief after a morning chock-full of Kaitlynn.

"Wait. We should sit with Allison and Tahira," Kaitlynn said, touching Ariana's arm.

Kaitlynn tilted her head toward the two girls, who were sitting at a small table near the door. Ariana hesitated, but she knew Kaitlynn was right. If anyone from Stone and Grave was watching—and Ariana knew that they always were—they would appreciate her and Kaitlynn sitting with the rest of their tap class. Ariana sighed and resigned herself to unpleasant company. Impressing Stone and Grave was worth a painful meal or two.

"Okay," she said. As she walked ahead of Kaitlynn, she saw her roommate's look of bemusement over having been agreed with so easily.

"Hey," Ariana said, sliding into the empty seat next to Allison. The girl's tall frame was slumped in her chair, and her blue-and-gold APH tie was loosely knotted over her light blue shirt. Her short blond curls were tucked behind her ears in a careless way, and her fingernails had been bitten down to nubs. Still, she was one of the more stunning girls in the room.

Allison and Tahira shot each other an intrigued look as Kaitlynn took the chair next to Tahira.

"Ladies," Kaitlynn said by way of greeting.

"How are you?" Tahira asked Ariana with surprisingly genuine interest. Her appearance was also surprisingly understated. Normally the girl managed to make her APH uniform as skimpy as possible, but today her shirt had only two buttons undone and she wore less eye makeup than usual.

"Okay, I guess. Not great," Ariana replied, lifting a shoulder. "You?"

"It's really weird around here without her," Tahira said, her dark eyes guarded. "Who am I going to spar with from now on?"

Even though Tahira and Allison hadn't liked Brigit much, Ariana knew they had been affected by her tragic death. Everyone had.

The waiter approached and took their breakfast order, scribbling down Tahira's very specific dietary instructions and raising an eyebrow when Ariana asked for extra butter and syrup with her pancakes. Now was definitely the time to indulge in comfort food.

"So," Ariana said, folding her arms on the table as the waiter scurried off.

"So," Tahira replied, taking a breath.

They all looked at one another as if they didn't know where or how to start having a normal conversation.

Across the room, Quinn, a pretty, preppy sophomore, approached, and her two friends, Jessica and Melanie, delivered steaming lattes to Lexa, Soomie, and Maria. At the beginning of the year Ariana had thought the sophomores' constant errand running was just general cool-senior worship, but now she realized that Quinn and the other girls were probably also gunning for spots in Stone and Grave next year—trying to impress the girls whom they assumed were members.

"What do we think about Hell Week?" Ariana asked quietly, deciding to go with the one topic they all had in common. She glanced around to make sure no one was listening. At the next table, a pair of boys intensely scribbled out their calculus homework, and behind Ariana a group of freshman girls gabbed about Halloween costumes. "I assumed it was going to start the night of the NoBash, since we were all supposed to have our tasks completed by then, but then . . ."

"Do you think they're still going to have it?" Allison shifted in her seat. "I mean, considering?" She cast a brief look toward Ariana's usual table and Ariana automatically followed suit. Soomie picked at her food while Lexa and Maria watched the taps with interest. Snagged,

Maria looked away, but Lexa simply lifted her fingers in a wave, not at all embarrassed about being caught.

"Of course they are," Tahira whispered. "This is Stone and Grave. Hundreds of years of tradition can't just be ignored because of one—"

She stopped there and blushed as she looked down at her untouched silverware. For a moment, no one spoke. Ariana wondered if the sickened feeling in her heart would ever go away.

"So, Tahira . . . did you ever complete your task?" Ariana asked. Each pledge had been assigned a task to complete by the NoBash.

"Why? Are you suddenly concerned I won't get in?" Tahira asked facetiously. Of course, both Tahira and Ariana knew why Ariana was really asking. Tahira's task was to humiliate a donor, and she'd threatened to humiliate Ariana. Briana Leigh's family had donated hundreds of thousands of dollars to the school to get her in.

"Just curious," Ariana said, casually lifting her shoulders as their food arrived. Her plate of pancakes was steaming hot and smelled deliciously buttery. Ariana's stomach grumbled for the first time in more than a week. Mourning for Brigit had pretty much destroyed her appetite, but now that she had a plan in mind, she was more than ready to make up for lost time. "Did you find a donor to humiliate?"

Tahira daintily speared a grape with her fork. "Yes, I did."

"You told her what your task was?" Allison gasped, leaning forward. "You wouldn't even tell me!"

"Calm it, Al," Tahira said tersely. "I had my reasons."

Allison dropped back in her chair and crossed her arms over her chest to mope.

"Well? What'd you do?" Kaitlynn asked, leaning an elbow on the table. She'd ordered a bagel and lox, which so far had gone untouched. "Who'd you humiliate?"

"Well, you know Malaya was at the NoBash?" Tahira said, placing her fork down. "She was talking to all of these dignitaries and gurus and whatnot, so I went over and started asking her really specific questions about Buddhism, since that's supposed to be her new big obsession and everything," she said, waving a hand around dismissively.

"I thought she was into kabbalah." Allison took a large bite of her English muffin.

"Yeah. That was during her *last* world tour," Tahira said, rolling her eyes. "Anyway, of course she didn't actually know anything about Buddhism even though she's been quoted as saying it changed her life and all that crap," Tahira said. "She was so embarrassed, she faked a phone call from one of her kids and left the party."

Kaitlynn and Allison laughed.

"Well, good. I'm glad you got it done in time," Ariana said.

"Uh, thanks?" Tahira replied dubiously. "I just hope someone from Stone and Grave was paying attention," she whispered, reaching for her coffee cup. "It all happened right before . . ."

"Right before they found Brigit?" Kaitlynn said.

Ariana took a deep breath and reached for the juice. She couldn't let Kaitlynn see how much just talking about Brigit affected her.

"I don't even know if our tasks are going to matter anymore," Kaitlynn said, slathering cream cheese on her bagel.

"What? Why wouldn't they?" Allison asked.

Kaitlynn shrugged as she chewed and wiped a bit of cheese from her fingers onto her linen napkin.

"Well, I mean, they said there were four open spots . . . ," she said, keeping her voice down. She said it as if it had just occurred to her recently—as if she was thinking out loud—when, in fact, she had already killed someone based on her logic.

Tahira swallowed so hard that Ariana heard the gulp. "And now there are four of us."

Allison and Tahira looked at one another, then at Ariana, who found herself liking them for the first time since she'd met them more than a month ago. At least they had the decency to appear scandalized and depressed over what Kaitlynn had just said, while Kaitlynn sipped her orange juice and looked to be about three seconds away from humming a jaunty tune.

"Well, I for one will be happy if we do all get in," Ariana said, forcing a chipper tone into her voice.

"You will?" Kaitlynn said, clearly surprised.

"Yes," Ariana replied. "I mean, after everything that's happened . . . it would be nice if something positive came out of it. Who knows? Maybe Hell Week will bond us somehow. Maybe, by the end of it, we'll all be friends."

Tahira and Allison glanced at each other.

"I think Brigit would have liked that," Ariana added, looking at Kaitlynn.

For the first time in a long time, Kaitlynn seemed to be at a loss, like she had no idea what game Ariana was playing.

Which was just the way Ariana liked it.

LIFE IS CRAZY

Late Monday evening, Ariana held a tennis ball in her right hand. She thought of Brigit and squeezed. She thought of Kaitlynn and squeezed even harder, gritting her teeth, holding her breath, clenching her arm muscles. She thought of Brigit falling, Brigit screaming, Brigit's neck breaking as she hit the cold, hard floor, and she reached back and hurled the tennis ball at the wall of her dorm room. It smacked into the Monet poster Kaitlynn had hung over her bed, causing a slight tear in one of the center flowers before ricocheting across the room and taking out the perfume bottles atop Ariana's dresser. As a few more items crashed to the floor, Ariana grabbed another ball from her tennis bag and hurled it, widening the tear.

If only she had walked in on Brigit and Kaitlynn before it had happened. Ariana was sure she could have stopped it.

She hurled another ball. It missed the poster completely, bounced wide, and came to rest just inside Kaitlynn's open closet.

She could have overpowered Kaitlynn and then it would have been Kaitlynn's body that was found at the foot of the stairs, not Brigit's.

Another ball. The tear reached the top of the poster.

Ariana reached for a fifth, but there were none left. She closed her eyes, leaned back in her desk chair, and breathed.

She imagined her and Brigit clinging to each other after Kaitlynn's fall, still scared by the confrontation—the near miss—but grateful to be alive. Imagined telling the Norwegian guard what had happened—that "Lillian" had tried to kill the princess and "Ana" had saved the day.

But the fantasy stopped there. Ariana blinked and sat up straight. If Kaitlynn had died that night, in such a public way, it would have taken about five seconds for the authorities to find out that she wasn't a girl named Lillian Oswald at all—that she was in fact Kaitlynn Nottingham, escaped convict. And if they figured that out, it would have taken them about five more seconds to ID Ariana. Okay, maybe ten, but still. Even if Brigit were alive and Kaitlynn were dead, it would have been all over for Ariana.

Ariana turned toward her desk and slammed her heavy U.S. government book shut, cursing under her breath. It seemed as if she wouldn't be getting any studying done tonight, which sucked considering Kaitlynn was going to be out at an away soccer game all evening. Ariana hadn't even known Kaitlynn played soccer until she joined the team as her mandatory APH sport, but apparently the girl was good. She'd already been named a starter. Ariana wondered how many other secrets Kaitlynn was hiding, whether banal or harrowing.

She clutched her forearm in her fingers and squeezed, holding her breath as a hot wave of fury crashed through her.

Control, Ariana . . . control.

She closed her eyes and started to breathe.

In, one . . . two . . . three . . .

Out, one . . . two . . . three . . .

In, one . . . two . . . three . . .

Out, one . . . two . . . three . . .

There was a sudden knock at the door. With one last breath to steady her quaking nerves, Ariana got up. As soon as she opened the door, Palmer Liriano cupped her face in his hands and brought his full lips down on hers, backing her into the room again and slamming the door with a backward kick of his foot. Ariana giggled, the sound almost foreign to her own ears, and tripped backward, letting him lower her down onto her bed and settle in next to her, kissing her the entire time.

A few weeks ago, Palmer had broken up with Lexa so that he could go out with Ariana, but Ariana had insisted on keeping their relationship secret—at least until she could be certain that her new friend Lexa was truly over Palmer. On the night of the NoBash, Palmer had challenged Ariana about taking their relationship public, but he hadn't mentioned it since. So for the past week the two of them had been sneaking around as usual, stealing moments together after class or during study hours. These moments were Ariana's refuge and she cherished them like they were gold.

"Hello," Palmer said, finally parting his lips from hers.

He was so insanely handsome, with his jet-black hair and warm brown eyes, his tanned skin and easy smile, that sometimes it was almost impossible to tear her eyes off him.

"Hey," she replied with a grin. He trailed kisses down her neck and she placed her hand against his chest, feeling his muscles through the soft cotton of his T-shirt. "What would you have done if Lillian were here?"

Palmer's brow knit. "Kicked her out on her ass, of course," he said. "Nothing keeps me from you."

Ariana laughed at the visual. "How very chivalrous of you."

"I'm a chivalrous guy," he said jokingly. He ran a fingertip down her cheek, sending pleasant flutters through her chest. "So, what were you doing when I rudely interrupted?" Palmer leaned on his side and crooked his elbow under his head.

"Trying to study for our government quiz," Ariana replied, sitting up and gesturing at the book. It looked so massive and foreboding just sitting there.

"Trying?" he asked.

"Having a hard time concentrating," Ariana admitted, averting her eyes.

"Oh."

Palmer swung his legs over the side of the bed and got up. He leaned over her open laptop and scrolled through what few notes she had taken. "I can e-mail you my notes, if you want."

"Yeah?" Ariana said, standing up to face him. "That would be amazing." She reached for his hand and took it lightly in hers, toying with his fingers. "But . . . haven't you been distracted too? With the whole Brigit thing?"

A shadow passed over Palmer's handsome features. "Yeah, but that just means my notes are even better than usual. That's how I deal. By staying busy."

Ariana used to be that way too. Back at Easton Academy, whenever something bad happened, her grades only went up and her extracurriculars became her solace. What had changed? Why was she different now? Maybe it was because back then the bad things that had happened had seemed manageable. But now . . .

"Hey. Are you okay?" Palmer asked, reaching for her hand. "You just got sad."

Ariana attempted to smile. "Yeah. I just—"

There was a quick rap at the door and then Lexa walked in. Ariana dropped Palmer's hand, but stopped herself from springing away from him. She froze instead, gripping the back of the desk chair, realizing that moving away from Lexa's ex would just make her look even more guilty than she already did. Still, Lexa's eyes darted between Palmer and Ariana. Ariana's fingers tingled. Had she been too slow? Had Lexa seen?

"Hey, Lexa," Palmer said smoothly. "What's up?"

Lexa looked from Palmer to Ariana and back again. "Nothing . . . What's up with you?" She glanced around the room suspiciously. Her eyes paused briefly on Kaitlynn's torn poster.

"Not much." Palmer turned to Ariana. "So you'll e-mail me those notes, right?" he said, backing toward the door.

"Sure," Ariana said. "No problem. Glad I could help."

Palmer winked and smiled at Ariana as he slipped into the hallway and closed the door behind him. Ariana's heart fluttered around in her chest like a caged bird. If possible, she loved him even more for being so suave under pressure.

"Notes?" Lexa asked, raising her perfect eyebrows.

"Yeah. We have a quiz this week," Ariana said, closing her laptop so Lexa wouldn't see that her notes document was practically empty. "We figure between the two of us we may have absorbed most of the information."

Lexa nodded and took a couple of steps toward Kaitlynn's bed. "What happened?" she asked, gesturing at the poster. "Were you guys wrestling in here?" She laughed, but her eyes were flat and dead serious.

Ariana blushed. "Uh, no," she said lightly, rolling her eyes. "It was like that when I got here. I guess Lillian doesn't like that one anymore." She added a shrug for good measure, but silently cursed her own carelessness. Now she was going to have to run to the student store and replace the poster before Kaitlynn got home.

"Weird." Lexa sat down on the edge of Ariana's bed and Ariana perched on her desk chair, finally feeling the residual blush from her encounter with Palmer fading from her cheeks.

"So, what's up?" Ariana asked.

Lexa blew out a sigh. "I just needed to vent," she said finally. "I mean, if you've got a minute."

"That's what I'm here for," Ariana said with a smile, even though every cell in her body became tense. What, exactly, did Lexa want to vent about? Did it have to do with her and Palmer?

"It's my parents," Lexa said. Ariana's shoulders relaxed. She even felt a thrill over the fact that Lexa had come to her and not Maria or Soomie—over the proof of just how close she and Lexa had grown. "I just got off a conference call with Keiko and my mom's new assistant, Cassandra, trying to plan a time that all three of us can get together and have brunch. It was like a meeting of the U.N. Security Council or something. Just to have brunch with the folks."

"Well . . . it's good that they want to get together at all, right?" Ariana said, trying to find the positive angle.

"I guess." Lexa studied her nails. "Whatever. I'm sure they'll both have their own photographers present. Maybe I should hire one too." Then her eyes lit up and she sat up straight again. "You want to do it? It could be fun. You could be my very own paparazzo."

Ariana laughed. "Thanks for the offer, but I suck with a camera. Not to mention I'm not much of a stalker."

"Oh well. It was worth a try," Lexa joked. She looked Ariana in the eye, her smile softening. "Thanks."

"For what?" Ariana asked.

"Listening. I'm sure you don't want to hear about my family crap." Lexa averted her eyes and smoothed out one of the wrinkles in Ariana's bedspread.

Ariana swallowed hard, hoping Lexa couldn't somehow divine that Palmer had made those wrinkles. "Of course I do. That's what friends are for."

Lexa blushed and her smile widened. "Is it? I keep forgetting," she joked.

Ariana laughed.

"Anyway, there are other way more fun things to talk about," Lexa said, her green eyes sparkling.

"Like what?" Ariana asked.

"Like Halloween. Conrad came up with *the* best idea for our costume," Lexa said. "We're going as Heidi Klum and Seal."

Ariana laughed. "I love it! But isn't Connie a little bulky to be Seal?" Lexa's new boyfriend Conrad was built like a pro linebacker, with a thick neck, broad shoulders, and muscles to spare.

"He'll dress slim," Lexa replied. "And all I need is a blond wig, a short skirt, and a serious leg wax. What are you going as?"

"I don't know," Ariana said, feeling suddenly exhausted. "Halloween's never been my favorite holiday. I never really got the fun of dressing up."

"Oh, but you have to!" Lexa said. "You can't go to Soomie's party without a costume. Everyone's going all out. You know, for Brigit."

The name hung in the air between them. Ariana looked at Lexa, then quickly turned to gaze out the window. Old-school torchlights glowed all across the campus like a handful of low-hanging stars. Lexa sighed and leaned back on her hands.

"Was it wrong of us to convince Soomie to have the party? Everyone's still . . . I mean, *I'm* still spontaneously bursting into tears all the time. And Soomie's been so depressed," she said, squinting and chewing on her bottom lip. "Is it, I don't know . . . too soon to try to have fun?"

Ariana took a deep breath. "No. You guys were right. It's what she would have wanted. Maybe it'll cheer everyone up a little. I think if we do it right, it'll be good. It'll be like . . . keeping her spirit alive."

Lexa nodded slowly. There was a long moment of silence. "I really miss her."

"Me too," Ariana said, her heart heavy.

"I'm so glad you transferred here, Briana Leigh," Lexa said, reaching over to hug Ariana. Ariana stiffened at the use of her full fake name. Lexa had known the real Briana Leigh Covington when the two of them were kids, and every once in a while she would drop her full name, reminding Ariana of how fragile her assumed identity was. One slip and Lexa could realize she was an imposter. "Having you here and becoming friends again after all this time. It's like . . . I don't know . . . it makes me think life can't be that bad, you know?"

Ariana hugged Lexa back, staring blankly over her shoulder at the framed photo of Briana Leigh's ranch back in Texas—one of the personal items Briana Leigh's maid had mailed to her at the beginning of the school year. Ariana knew exactly how bad life could be. Her very presence here at APH, the very fact that she was walking around masquerading as Briana Leigh Covington, was the result of how bad life could be. And she knew that as long as Kaitlynn Nottingham was here, getting her way, life was only going to get worse.

NO GUARANTEES

Ariana hustled across campus on a still, cool Tuesday night, headed for the library, hoping that a change of scenery would help her concentrate on her homework. She was so stressed she didn't even take the time to notice the gorgeous shades of the changing leaves around her or turn her head at the sound of shouts and laughter from one of the dorms. She couldn't believe the number of assignments that had been piled on her that day. With all she had to deal with, schoolwork had fallen woefully low on her list of priorities. Which really wasn't going to cut it if she wanted to fulfill her lifelong dream of getting into Princeton.

A few yards away from the double-oak doors of the stately red-brick library, Ariana heard a crack, then an under-the-breath curse and the telltale crunch of leaves underfoot. She paused and looked around. There were a few people crisscrossing the campus, but no one near enough to be heard that distinctly. Someone was hiding nearby, watching her. A buzz of fear-tinged excitement raced through her and she clutched the strap on her bag, taking a deep breath and trying to appear calm. This was it. Hell Week was here.

A moment passed and suddenly, two dark figures sprang out of the bushes and threw a black hood over her head.

"Come with us," a gruff voice said in her ear.

Ariana didn't scream or struggle. Instead she concentrated on not tripping as two hands gripped her arms and hurried her forward. She took long, deliberate breaths, which wasn't easy given that her face was covered and the sour scent of mildew filled her nostrils. At first it seemed as if they were headed for the library, but then they took an abrupt turn, and another, and another, until she was completely confused and dizzy. By the time she heard a door creak open and was hurried awkwardly down a set of hard, shallow steps, Ariana was sweating profusely and panting unattractively. At the very bottom of the stairs, one of her two kidnappers tripped. She flew forward, but they caught her before she could fall flat on her face. The tripper muttered something unintelligible and they kept moving.

For one blissful moment, cool air rushed in around Ariana, but as she and her captors shuffled on, the atmosphere gradually grew warmer, and she could sense the glow of warm light through the tiny holes in the fabric of the hood. Her shoes made scratching sounds on the floor, as if she was walking across silty concrete. Suddenly, someone grabbed her, holding her in place.

"Don't move," a male voice growled in her ear.

Ariana bowed her head but said nothing. A shoulder knocked

hers and she almost tripped sideways. Somewhere off to her right, a guy cursed.

"Quiet, plebe!" a gravelly voice shouted.

Someone yanked something over Ariana's head. For a second she thought they were putting another hood atop the first one and the lack of air was stifling. But then, the sack was pulled down over her clothes and she realized it was a robe of some kind. It was thick, itchy, and suffocating and smelled of onion and mothballs and dust. Ariana breathed through her mouth as nimble fingers worked quickly to tie something around her waist. Then, mercifully, her hood was yanked off from behind.

Ariana took a deep breath. Her throat itched with a cough, but she held it in. She didn't want to appear weak in front of the members of Stone and Grave, all of whom were standing in front of her—a sea of black robes, faces obscured by silver and black masks. Surrounding the membership were shelves and shelves of books. Thousands of them lined the walls, stretching off into the darkness. The glow Ariana had sensed while still blindfolded emanated from a collection of black candles that littered every surface. Ariana glanced around and saw Kaitlynn standing directly to her left. Lined up next to her were Tahira, Allison, Landon, Adam, and the blond guy she'd seen talking to Christian at Brigit's memorial. These, apparently, were her male counterparts. All of them were wearing roughly hewn burlap robes over their clothes, and each was tied with a plain white rope belt. Ariana could feel the itchy material through her light wool coat, and sweat began to prickle under her arms. Whoever had removed her blindfold still stood behind her, and the knowledge that someone she couldn't see was hovering so close made the tiny hairs on the back of her neck stand on end.

"Welcome to the Tombs."

A broad, obviously male figure stepped away from the rest of the Stone and Grave membership. He was followed by a petite female member.

"Welcome to Stone and Grave," she said.

Ariana recognized their voices and statures. They were the same two Stone and Gravers who had greeted them in the woods on the night of their first kidnapping. The night they'd first found out they had been tapped. The guy's Stone and Grave name was Lear and the girl's was Miss Temple. Just as she was wondering if she'd ever find out who they really were, they both reached up and removed their hoods, then their masks.

Ariana's breath caught. Lear was none other than Lexa's boyfriend, the athletic, dark, and handsome Conrad Royce, and Miss Temple was April Corrigan, the intelligent, no-nonsense editor of the *Ash* literary magazine. April's red curls spilled out over her shoulders in stark contrast to the black velvet robe, and the candlelight was reflected in the lenses of her small tortoiseshell glasses.

"I am Lear," Conrad said, his deep voice reverberating through the room. "This is Miss Temple," he added, gesturing at April. "We will be your pledge educators."

Ariana pressed her lips together to keep from smiling to herself. She already had an in with both of her pledge educators. She sat next to

Conrad in English class and was the one who'd hooked Connie up with Lexa, and she and April had totally bonded at the *Ash* meetings.

"You have all completed your first task, and completed it admirably," April said, looking each of them in the eye with an imperious scowl. Her Irish accent came through loud and clear, and Ariana was impressed that she had been able to disguise it so well. "You have taken your first steps toward full membership in Stone and Grave."

Ariana felt a smile playing around her lips and struggled to keep a straight face.

"But your journey is just beginning," Conrad added, his voice deadly serious. He paced along the line of pledges, dwarfing even Landon, the tallest of the boys. "It's a journey that can reap for you the greatest rewards. Membership in Stone and Grave means power. It means prestige. It means success in anything and everything you wish to achieve. Your brothers and sisters in Stone and Grave will be there for you to celebrate your greatest triumphs, but even more important, they will be there to lift you up if ever you should fall." He paused, back at the center of the line, standing directly across from Ariana. "Membership in Stone and Grave means you will never want for a thing."

The rest of the Stone and Grave membership stood as still as statues, but Ariana couldn't help shifting from one foot to the other as a skitter of excitement went through her. She was so close she could taste it. *Princeton, here I come.*

"But it is not guaranteed," April added, ducking her chin as she gazed at them. "As you know, we have four open spots for female members, three for male . . . but that does not mean that we have to take all four women, or all three men."

Ariana's heart plummeted. She felt Kaitlynn tense up next to her. *Not guaranteed. Not guaranteed.*

Even with Brigit's death, their membership was not guaranteed.

"This is an exclusive society," Conrad said. "We are not about quantity, we are about quality. If you don't measure up, you don't get in. It's as simple as that. We'll take all of you . . . or some . . . or none."

A lump as hard as a rock formed in Ariana's throat and she suddenly felt the extreme heat coming off the candles. Kaitlynn had murdered Brigit to ensure herself a spot in Stone and Grave, but her spot was not ensured by Brigit's absence. No one's was.

Ariana's hand automatically gripped her forearm, her fingers cutting off all circulation as she squeezed. Brigit was dead for no reason. No reason. No reason at all. Ariana's vision started to prickle over with tiny gray dots. She was going to faint. Or worse. She had to get control. Now.

Just breathe, Ariana.

In, one . . . two . . . three . . .

Out, one . . . two . . . three . . .

Thick, waxy air filled Ariana's lungs and her vision slowly began to clear. She had to concentrate on her current purpose. She had to concentrate on Kaitlynn. Kaitlynn, who had to be freaking out right about now. Because Kaitlynn needed Stone and Grave even more than Ariana did. While Ariana had Briana Leigh Covington's past to build on, Kaitlynn had nothing. No money, no family, nothing. Her very identity was a complete fabrication. Ariana knew that Kaitlynn was hoping that Stone and Grave would offer her stability, a sort of de facto family—a network to rely on for money, places to stay, college recommendations—her whole future. Which was why she'd gone so far as to kill to get in.

Slowly, Ariana turned her head so that she could see Kaitlynn from the corner of her eye. Kaitlynn's skin looked sickly pale in the candlelight, like she was about to throw up. For a split second, Ariana's heart almost went out to her.

"Over the next two weeks you will be led through a series of tasks," April said, shaking her red curls back from her face. She pushed her glasses up on her nose and gave the pledges a no-nonsense glare. "And I want to be perfectly clear on this. When it comes to these tasks, failure is not an option."

Behind April and Conrad, the members of Stone and Grave stood still and hushed. This was a serious directive. If ever the pledges wanted to be standing on the other side of this ceremony, they had better not screw up.

"We will meet tomorrow night at midnight, on the steps of the chapel," Conrad said. "Don't be late."

With that, a hood was yanked over Ariana's head again, and she was unceremoniously dragged up the stairs with the rest of the pledges.

PROVE IT

Ariana was the first to arrive at the foot of the chapel steps on Wednesday night. There was no sign of Conrad or April. Tahira and Allison were on their way—she'd heard them gabbing in their room about what to wear as she'd left the dorm. The guys would probably be the last to arrive, because they'd want to look cool and blasé about the whole thing. But the person she was most curious about was Kaitlynn.

Kaitlynn, whom Ariana hadn't seen all day.

She'd been up and out of the room before Ariana's alarm had ever gone off and she'd been MIA ever since. During the two classes the two of them shared, her desk had remained vacant and she hadn't shown up for any of the day's meals. By the time the dinner dishes were cleared, Ariana had started to suspect that Kaitlynn was gone for good.

Was it even possible? Had the news that her spot in Stone and Grave was not guaranteed sent her over the edge? Maybe she'd taken what was left of her money and gone off to start a new life. Ariana knew the very prospect should have sent her screaming gleefully across campus, turning cartwheels and hugging every person she met, but instead she felt an odd sense of disappointment.

A cold breeze tossed a yellow leaf across Ariana's foot. She looked down at it as it blew off into the night, and sighed.

"You're early."

Ariana whipped around, heart in her throat. Kaitlynn was standing directly behind her.

"You're here!" Ariana squealed. She threw her arms around Kaitlynn's neck and squeezed.

"Okay. What was that?" Kaitlynn asked when Ariana released her. There were dark circles under Kaitlynn's eyes and her short blond hair was frizzy and unkempt. She wore her black wool coat over jeans, and her sneakers were caked with mud.

"Where have you been all day?" Ariana asked under her breath. From the corner of her eye, she saw Tahira and Allison tromping down the hill from Privilege House, dressed in black from head to toe. Adam and Landon were close behind.

"Why? Were you worried about me?" Kaitlynn cocked an eyebrow.

"Yeah. I was," Ariana said under her breath. "I wanted to talk to you about the meeting last night," she said, tugging her coat closer to her against the cold. "I'm sure you were as freaked as I was by this whole no-guarantee thing."

Kaitlynn avoided Ariana's gaze, looking down at the ground and shoving her hands into the pockets of her coat. "You were freaked?" she said dubiously. "Don't you mean pissed?"

Ariana clenched her jaw for a moment and took a deep breath. "Why? Because of Brigit?"

Was that why Kaitlynn had stayed away all day?

Kaitlynn simply stared. "Aren't you?"

Blowing out a sigh, Ariana tugged her wool gloves out of her pockets and pulled them on. "Look, what's done is done. But I thought about what you said the other morning and I realized something."

"What?"

Ariana swallowed hard. The others were fast approaching. This conversation had to get where she needed it to go and she needed it to get there fast. "Brigit's gone. I can't bring her back. But you and me . . . we're still here. And you were right. We were best friends once."

Kaitlynn eyed Ariana with doubt. She turned slightly away from Ariana, as if she wanted to make sure there was no one behind her, ready to pounce and announce the joke was on her.

"Maybe we can be friends again," Ariana said with a small smile. "At least, I'm willing to try."

Kaitlynn narrowed her eyes and faced Ariana again. She opened her mouth to speak, but at that moment Tahira and Allison arrived.

"Hey there," Tahira said, tossing her long black hair over her shoulder. "Any idea what we're doing here?"

"None whatsoever," Ariana replied, trying not to sound as irritated as she felt at being interrupted.

The guys stepped up behind them, just as the blond boy from last night's ceremony arrived from the opposite direction. Ariana gazed past him, her brow knit, wondering where else he could have been coming from at such an hour. All of them lived in Privilege House, and the class and administration buildings had been closed since dinner.

"Evening, ladies," he said, nodding at them. "Gents."

"You guys know Jasper, right?" Landon knocked fists with him without waiting for a response.

Jasper smiled at Ariana as he rolled up onto his toes and back down to his heels again. There was something about his blatant stare that irked Ariana, and she looked away.

"It's a little weird that they picked such a wide-open spot for this, isn't it?" Tahira said, lifting her shoulders as she shivered. "Anyone could look out a window and see us."

"Ah, but it proves that Stone and Grave isn't afraid of anything," Jasper replied. "All part of their mystique."

"Well, whatever we're doing, I hope it doesn't take too long," Adam said, his brown curls tossed by the breeze. There were dark circles under his eyes, and he had a scrape on his lower cheek where he'd clearly cut himself shaving. "I have to work first thing in the morning."

One of a few scholarship students at Atherton-Pryce Hall, Adam was working off part of his tuition by acting as a student aide to the teachers in the history department.

"Dude. Whatever this is, it's way more important than work,"

Landon said, tossing his long bangs off his face. They fell right back where they'd been.

"Says the guy with seven-figure royalty checks rolling in every other month," Adam said flatly, earning a round of laughter from the group.

"Welcome, pledges."

Ariana whirled around, the moment of levity interrupted by the staid tone of Conrad's voice. Lear and Miss Temple had appeared on the chapel steps as if from nowhere. They both wore long black coats over their clothes, and Conrad carried a few black cotton bags. Ariana's heart started to pound from nerves.

"Tonight's test is a scavenger hunt," April explained as Conrad walked down the steps toward them. "Inside these bags is a list of things you are to find on campus, along with a camera so you can take a photo of each item."

Conrad handed one bag to each of the pledges. Ariana clutched the straps of hers, itching to get started. She glanced inside and spied a tiny silver digital camera and a thick card, but she couldn't make out a word on the list.

"Each list is different, and each of you must find every item on your list," April continued. "Once you've photographed all the items, you will bring the camera back here for inspection."

Conrad handed out the last bag and rejoined her on the steps. "This task is to be completed in a timely fashion," he warned. "Miss Temple and I will be waiting here, and believe me when I say neither of us wants to be up all night."

"And here's a little added motivation for you," April said. "Whoever returns last, loses."

"And you don't want to know what happens if you lose," Conrad said, his voice sending waves of dread through Ariana. She glanced at Kaitlynn, who shot her the briefest of looks before retraining her eyes on Conrad. Tahira and Allison were clutching hands, knees bent, as if they were waiting for some sort of starting gun to go off.

"Well? What are you waiting for?" April said. "Go!"

Ariana shoved her hand into the bag and whipped out the white card. It wasn't a simple laundry list of items. Each one was a riddle that first needed to be solved.

1. My sentries stand two feet tall.
2. I sit where the angels weep.
3. A rose by any other name.

Ariana groaned. This was going to take forever.

Tahira and Allison turned and started off across campus arm-in-arm, reading over each other's lists and starting to work out the clues. Clearly, they were going to complete this task together. Kaitlynn, meanwhile, was staring down at her card, her camera dangling from her wrist by its strap, one hand covering her mouth as her forehead wrinkled in concentration.

"I don't know what half of this stuff even *is*," Kaitlynn said under her breath.

Ariana walked over and glanced at her list. "I do."

"You do?" Kaitlynn asked doubtfully. "How? You've only been here a week longer than I have."

"But I spent the two weeks before I came here memorizing everything there is to know about this school," Ariana said, looping her arm around Kaitlynn's, mimicking Tahira and Allison. "Come on. We can help each other."

She tugged Kaitlynn away from the steps, but Kaitlynn didn't move. She stood so still, in fact, that Ariana almost tripped herself. "You want to help me," Kaitlynn said, her tone disbelieving.

"Isn't that what friends do?" Ariana asked innocently. "Now come on. We'd better get started before we waste any more time."

She glanced over her shoulder and sure enough, Conrad and April were glaring down at them.

"Ticktock, ladies," April said, tapping her watch.

Kaitlynn sighed and looked at Ariana. "If you sabotage me, I am not going to be happy."

Ariana looped her arm around Kaitlynn's and started for the fountain at the center of campus. "Believe me, Lily, the last thing I want right now is for you to be unhappy."

DISMISSED

"'A rose by any other name.' What does that mean?" Ariana said through her teeth.

The frustration and panic mounted inside her chest as she gazed around campus, as if the answer would jump out at her from behind one of the arched doorways or from underneath a dormer window. Ariana had single-handedly solved every other clue on both their lists while Kaitlynn had been next to useless. So why was she coming up blank now, when it mattered most?

Perhaps it was the shock over the fact that Kaitlynn's list was complete and she was still there trying to help Ariana, instead of hauling ass back to the chapel with her camera full of photos to show Lear and Miss Temple how well she'd done. Why? Why, for the first time in her life, was Kaitlynn not focused completely on herself?

"Okay . . . okay, is there a rose garden on campus?" Kaitlynn asked, holding her palms up. Her camera lay in one hand, while her black cotton bag dangled from the other. She curled the fingers of her free hand into a fist and blew into it. With each passing moment the air seemed to grow colder and colder.

"No. There aren't even any rosebushes in the topiary garden," Ariana said, bringing her gloved hand to her forehead. "What else could be called a rose?"

"Maybe we're thinking too literally," Kaitlynn said. She shoved her hands, camera and all, under her arms and chewed on the inside of her cheek as she looked around. Her eyes fell on Cornwall House, one of the girls' dorms. "Wait a minute! All the buildings have names, right? Are any of them named Rose? Or maybe some other flower? Since it's a rose by any other name . . ."

Ariana's memory prickled with a vague heat.

She took a few steps away from Kaitlynn, struggling to piece it together. It was something she'd read in the APH handbook all those weeks ago when she was staying at the Philmore Hotel on Lake Page, getting ready to start her new life as Briana Leigh Covington. She closed her eyes and tried to see the words. "The Winifred R. Sherman Computer Annex . . . Winifred R. Sherman. Her maiden name was Winifred Rose!"

"That's gotta be it!" Kaitlynn said, her eyes wide with glee. "Once she got married, she had *another* name!"

"Let's go!"

The annex was connected to the library. Ariana turned and ran for the building at a sprint, Kaitlynn right at her side. Ariana's cold feet protested with tingly pain at each step. As she rounded the corner at the north end, she spotted the annex's cornerstone and felt a rush of elation. Just above the date, 1948, there was a small but elegant rose etched into the stone. Ariana crouched in front of the stone, turned on the flash, and snapped the picture.

"Got it?" Kaitlynn asked as Ariana stood up to check the photo on the display screen.

"Got it."

Ariana grabbed Kaitlynn's hand, and together they raced across campus to the chapel. As Ariana neared, she could see a few figures standing around the steps and her heart clenched. What if everyone was already back? What if they were too late? Running had never been her favorite thing, but she upped her speed, sprinting the last few steps. She doubled over as she handed her camera to Conrad, gasping for breath. Kaitlynn gave hers to April. They both stood back as their pledge educators scrolled through the photos saved on their cameras.

"You took long enough," Tahira joked as Ariana and Kaitlynn joined her and Alison at the bottom of the stairs. Jasper was there too, and he inclined his head in Ariana's direction. She blushed and looked away.

"We had a couple of tough ones," Ariana said breathlessly, glancing at Kaitlynn. At least the run had warmed her up a bit. "I couldn't have done it without Lily's help."

It wasn't exactly true—except, possibly, for the last clue—but she knew that Kaitlynn would appreciate the compliment.

Allison checked her watch. "Where are Landon and Adam? I'm starting to freeze."

Then, as if on cue, Ariana saw Landon running toward them from the direction of the boathouse. At the same time, Adam appeared from behind the dining hall, sprinting as if his life depended on it.

Ariana's heart was in her throat as the two boys streaked toward the chapel, wondering who was going to make it there first, and what would happen to the other. Landon's foot hit the bottom stair three seconds before Adam's. The difference was so negligible, Ariana was certain it wouldn't matter. They handed their cameras over, and April and Conrad scrolled through the photos. Both breathless, Landon and Adam joined the other pledges at the base of the steps.

"Good work," Conrad said, looking up. "Each of you has completed your scavenger hunt lists."

Ariana looked at the others and grinned. Their relief was palpable.

"Unfortunately, Adam, you were the last to return with your camera," April said.

The smile dropped from Adam's face, his chest still heaving up and down from the run. Conrad walked slowly down the steps and stood in front of him, looking down his nose at the far smaller boy. Ariana held her breath, as did everyone around her.

"You're out," Conrad said.

"What?" Adam squeaked.

"I'm sorry. You are no longer a candidate for membership," Conrad said. "Leave. Now."

Ariana's mind whirled. She couldn't believe that Conrad—jovial, devil-may-care Conrad—could be so blunt and cruel. Adam didn't move. It was like he was waiting for the punch line. Conrad took a step closer so that Adam's nose was practically buried in his shoulder.

"*Now,*" he repeated.

Ariana flinched. Adam glanced uncertainly at the other taps, as if he thought one of them might speak up for him. When no one did, he took a shaky step back.

"Fine," he said with a tense laugh. "I don't need this crap anyway."

Then he turned his back on their silence and walked away quickly, his head held high as he disappeared into the night. April picked up a stack of packages wrapped in plain brown paper, which hadn't been there when the scavenger hunt began. She descended the stairs lightly, as if nothing out of the ordinary had just happened, but Ariana knew the other pledges felt as thrown off as she did. How could the Stone and Grave eliminate Adam so cavalierly? He was a nice guy—smart, athletic, promising. And now he was out just because he was three seconds slower at a sprint than Landon?

"These are your Stone and Grave handbooks," April explained, handing one package to each of them. The crisp, brown wrapping paper crackled as Ariana's fingers gripped the book. "Inside you will find vital information on Atherton-Pryce Hall and its current students and faculty. Your job is to memorize every fact within its pages," April instructed. "Starting tomorrow, you may be quizzed at any given moment by any member of Stone and Grave, and I urge you to be ready with the correct answers, or the results will not be pretty."

She stepped up next to Conrad.

"I suggest you not test us on this," she said. "As I believe we've just proven, everyone is expendable."

Ariana blinked. April said those awful words so sweetly—the same words Ariana had heard in Kaitlynn's veiled threat—it somehow made the threat that much more real.

"You are dismissed," Conrad said.

Ariana turned on shaky knees and fell into step with Kaitlynn. "Well. That was harsh."

Kaitlynn said nothing. She tucked her package under her folded arms and quickened her steps.

"So, want to stay up together and study this?" Ariana said, lifting her own package. "We can quiz each other."

"I can't believe they just did that," Kaitlynn muttered, staring straight ahead. "I can't believe they just booted Adam like that. They didn't even give him a chance."

"Right. Which is all the more reason for us to study together," Ariana said, struggling to keep pace with her roommate. "Two heads are better than one and all that."

"Whatever," Kaitlynn said under her breath. "Right now I'm thinking it's every man for himself."

Ariana stopped in her tracks, stunned. Did Kaitlynn not realize that she wouldn't have finished three-quarters of her scavenger hunt list if not for Ariana's help? Where was her thank-you? Where was the acknowledgment of her friendship? Kaitlynn speed-walked ahead so that soon the chasm between them was too wide to cross. It was all Ariana could do to keep from hurling her handbook at the girl's retreating head.

"She's an interesting one."

Ariana looked up to find Jasper pausing next to her. He narrowed his blue eyes at her and offered his hand. "Jasper Montgomery," he said. "Of the Louisiana Montgomerys."

"Ana Covington," she replied, briefly grasping his hand. "Of the

Texas Covingtons," she added in a slightly mocking tone.

He held her gaze for a long moment—so long that Ariana felt a blush rise to her cheeks. She started walking again.

"I'll stay up and study with you, if you like," Jasper said, matching her pace.

"Thanks, but I'm good," Ariana replied.

"I've no doubt you are," Jasper said in a teasing way. "But the offer remains just the same."

Ariana pursed her lips. There was nothing that disgusted her more than a double entendre from a boy she barely knew. But when she looked up at Jasper to tell him off, there was no leer in his eyes, just a joking spark.

"Maybe another time," she said. "Right now I'd like to get some sleep. I'll wake up early and study then."

"Suit yourself. Me?" he said with a smirk as they reached the door to Privilege House. "I'll have this thing memorized by first light."

Jasper waved his electronic key in front of the lock and held the door open for her. Ariana paused. There were a thousand comebacks on her lips, but for some reason she didn't feel like dropping them. Maybe she was just exhausted from the scavenger hunt. Or still thrown from Adam's unceremonious fall. Or frustrated by Kaitlynn's refusal to trust her. Whatever the case, she felt thrown and off her game. And suddenly all she wanted to do was get away from Jasper as quickly as possible and put this whole exasperating night behind her.

"Thanks," she said as she slipped past him into the dorm.

"Pleasure's mine," he replied with a grin.

COWS

Something was after her. Something lurking in the woods. Ariana heard a crack, a creak, a moan, and then something reached for her in the dark, its cold and slimy fingers trailing over her bare shoulder. Stifling a scream, she ran. She ran as hard and as fast as she could, feeling the thing gaining on her in the pitch-black night. Breathing down her neck. Panting hot and wet and evil. She tried to run, but her legs wouldn't move. They were too heavy. Impossibly heavy. She looked down at her feet and they were mired in muck. Ankle-deep in muddy, rocky sludge.

And the thing kept gaining. Fear gripped Ariana's heart. She held her breath and struggled forward. Pushing and pulling and grasping and straining until finally she pried her feet free. With one glance back over her shoulder, Ariana flew forward and slammed right into the side of . . .

A cow?

The huge brown animal looked back at her, sniffed in a bored, indignant way, and let out a loud moo.

Ariana sat up with a start, her hand on her chest. Her heart was pounding a mile a minute, but she was safe. Safe in her bed in Privilege House. There was nothing coming for her. At least not right now. It had all been a dream.

Then Ariana heard another moo. She glanced over at Kaitlynn, who was lifting her head out from under her pillow.

"What the hell was that?" Kaitlynn asked, blinking rapidly. Her blond hair stuck up straight from her head with static.

"It sounded . . . like a cow," Ariana replied, wiping the last vestiges of sleep from her eyes with her fingertips.

She flung her sheets and blanket off her legs. As she tiptoed over to the door, there was another moo, this time unmistakable, followed by a crash. Then Tahira screamed and Kaitlynn was out of bed like a shot, gripping Ariana's arm.

So much for every man for himself.

The door across the way slammed. Ariana put her hand on the doorknob.

"What're you doing?" Kaitlynn whispered.

"We have to see what's going on, don't we?" Ariana whispered back.

"No," Kaitlynn replied. "I say we just get back into bed and let someone else handle it."

Ariana looked at her roommate over her shoulder, raising one eyebrow. "Oh, so suddenly you're no longer up for taking matters into your own hands?"

Kaitlynn rolled her eyes. "Fine. Whatever. But I'm staying behind you."

Typical.

Ariana took a deep breath, held it, and yanked the door open. The flank of a spotted cow stared her right in the face.

"Omigod!" Kaitlynn shouted, springing backward.

Ariana heard a tearing sound and leaned out the door. The cow had a big square of the maize-colored carpet rolling around in its maw. "It's eating the rug!"

"What is all the noise about?" Lexa said, cinching her red robe around her waist as she came around the corner. She stopped in her tracks and her eyes widened. Her brown hair was all knotted on one side, and there was mascara smudged beneath her eyes. "Um, Ana? Why is there a cow outside your room?"

Before Ariana could answer, there was another scream on the other side of the floor. Soomie came running into view, her dark hair all knotted on one side.

"Omigod! There's another one!" she shouted, backing away from Ariana's cow.

"Where's the other one?" Ariana asked.

"In the common area," Soomie said, her jaw quivering as she pointed. "It's chewing on the couch!"

"Okay. It's okay," Ariana said in a soothing voice. "We'll take care of this. Just . . . go back to your room."

Soomie didn't have to be asked twice. She disappeared and two seconds later, her door slammed.

"We're going to take care of this?" Kaitlynn said, letting her hands slap down at her sides. "How, exactly?"

Ariana screwed her lips up. "I'm not really sure." She took a deep breath and smacked the cow hard on the flank. "All right, lady. Get in there and join your friend. Hiya! Come on now!"

The cow looked back at her and snorted, but moved along. Just as it was ambling its way into the common room, the elevator pinged and Palmer and Landon raced out, both wearing boxer shorts and T-shirts.

"You have cows too!" Palmer shouted, his eyes nearly popping out of his head. The guys lived in A tower—nicknamed Alpha—on the opposite side of Privilege House. To access the B tower—or Bella—they had to go all the way to the lobby in the A elevator, switch to the B elevator, and come back up.

"Why? How many do you have?" Ariana asked, crossing her arms over her nightgown, hoping she didn't look as disheveled and unattractive as Lexa did.

"Two! They completely destroyed the plasma in the common room." Palmer pressed himself flat against the wall of the hallway and peeked around the corner into the common area, as if one of the cows might be wielding a handgun.

"And they ate all the PSP games," Landon added.

Palmer turned again and looked past Ariana at Lexa, who slowly approaching. "Tsang," he said. "It has to be."

"But you only pulled the coconut prank in retaliation for the nail and hair thing," Lexa said, lifting a palm toward Palmer. "I thought that was more than fair as far as a reprisal goes."

Martin Tsang was a member of one of the other two secret societies on campus, the Fellows. Lexa had pegged him and his secret society for a series of midnight attacks that had taken place inside Privilege House, and Palmer had retaliated by filling Tsang's room with coconuts. Only Ariana and Kaitlynn knew that Kaitlynn was the one responsible for the attacks, so as far as the Fellows were concerned, Stone and Grave had fired the first shot of a prank war. This, clearly, was *their* idea of a reprisal.

Ariana noticed that both Palmer and Lexa were careful not to mention the Fellows out loud in mixed company, even though they knew that she, Kaitlynn, and Landon were all taps.

The four of them inched over to the open corner of the common area, sticking close together, and watched as the cows went to town on the velvet couch. Kaitlynn, meanwhile, hung back in the doorway of her and Ariana's room, listening, but clearly too freaked to come out.

"How did they even get these things up here?" Lexa asked.

"Very quietly," Landon said, scratching at the back of his neck, beneath his long, shaggy hair.

"Well . . . how are we supposed to get them out?" Lexa asked.

"Call Animal Control," Ariana replied, lifting her shoulders.

"I'll bet this'll be a first for them," Palmer said with a short laugh.

Just then, the spotted cow lifted its tail and relieved itself all over the common room floor. The stench was instant, and so vile that it stung Ariana's eyes. She dry-heaved and slapped a hand over her mouth.

"What the hell did they feed that thing?" Ariana asked through her fingers.

"Omigod," Lexa said, covering her face and turning away.

"That is just *wrong*," Landon added, covering his mouth and nose as well.

"Call Animal Control and then burn this place down!" Palmer said, his face screwed up in disgust.

"I am going to *kill* Martin Tsang!" Lexa shouted, running back to her room and slamming the door.

Palmer looked at Landon and Ariana, breathed through his mouth, and placed his hands on his hips. "This. Is. War."

BRILLIANT PLAN

"What a day," Maria said as she settled onto a settee at the Hill that night. It was a gorgeous fall evening, slightly warm with the sun still glowing off the brightly colored leaves outside. Most of the glass doors and windows of the junior/senior lounge were thrown open to let the fresh air in. Maria sucked down half of her espresso, a breeze teasing the wisps of brown hair around her face.

"Please. You never even saw the cows," Ariana said as she and Kaitlynn sat down across from her at the marble coffee table.

"That's because a smart girl knows when to stay inside," Maria replied with a smirk.

"Well, we have to do something and we have to do it fast," Lexa said, dropping down in a high-backed chair. "I know Martin Tsang is behind this. He's been walking around with that stupid grin on his face all day."

She glanced over her left shoulder to where, a few tables away,

Martin and some of his friends were noshing on cookies and laughing it up. Martin noticed them looking and laughed even harder.

"We can't let him think he's won," Lexa said with a shudder, facing forward again. "You can't just walk into Privilege House and defile the place."

"Exactly," Palmer said, coming up behind Lexa with Landon, Jasper, Conrad, and Tahira's boyfriend, Rob, in tow. "Which is why we're going to retaliate. Tonight."

Ariana and Palmer exchanged a glance, and Palmer gave her a private smile as the guys squeezed in around the table. Jasper took a seat next to Ariana on the couch, forcing her closer to Kaitlynn's side. Ariana wished that Palmer could have sat there instead—that they could have just come out and told everyone they were together already—but now hardly seemed like the moment. Landon dropped down on the end of Maria's settee and she gave him a brief, private smile. It made Ariana feel better to be reminded that she wasn't the only one engaged in a secret relationship around here. Ariana wondered what Maria would have done if Landon had been two seconds behind Adam during the scavenger hunt, rather than the other way around. She was sure that her friend was in Stone and Grave, and that she wanted her boyfriend to get in too. Would she have had enough—or any—pull to save him?

Ariana watched Palmer as he pulled over another chair and sat next to Lexa. She had a hunch that Palmer wasn't just a member but was the president of the Atherton-Pryce Hall chapter of Stone and Grave. It made sense, considering he was president of the student body, captain of the gold team during welcome week, and the person everyone looked up to around here. Would *he* have been able to save *her* if she had been the last to complete her task?

"So do you guys have a plan?" Lexa asked, taking a sip of her coffee.

Palmer bit his lip. "Uh . . . no. You?"

There were blank stares all around. A pair of senior girls walked by on their way up to the coffee counter, fresh from a workout and wearing their APH Track hoodies. Ariana smiled at their retreating forms, recalling one of her own greatest all-time pranks—one she'd pulled on a bitchy classmate back when she was a freshman at Easton.

Before she could announce the idea, Kaitlynn leaned forward and looked around at the group. "Come on. Someone here must have pulled a good prank back in grade school," she said. "Something we can use as inspiration."

"Lily, what about that story you told me last week?" Ariana said, looking Kaitlynn in the eye. "That prank you pulled at your old school?"

Kaitlynn went wide-eyed, like a deer in headlights. "Which prank was that?" she asked Ariana. "I've pulled off so many, it's hard to remember which ones I've bragged about," she joked casually, looking around at the others.

"The one with the gum?" Ariana replied. "It'd be perfect!"

"Oh, right! The gum prank!" Kaitlynn said, faking a laugh.

Lexa raised one eyebrow. "Come on girls, spill."

"You tell it," Kaitlynn said, nudging Ariana's knee.

"God, Lily. You're so modest." Ariana sat forward, giddy as all eyes turned on her. This was already working like a charm. "Back at Lily's old school, there was this girl who always wore hoodies. Every day, it was the same hoodie in a different color, and whenever she stepped outside, she would lift the hood over her hair."

Maria drained the rest of her espresso and leaned in with interest.

"It was totally ridiculous," Kaitlynn chimed in, playing along now as if the story truly was hers. "That silhouette did nothing for her."

Maria smirked.

"So one day in English class, Lily sat behind her, chewed up a nice, big wad of gum, and placed it in her hood," Ariana said.

"No!" Lexa cried.

"Yes!" Ariana replied.

"My friends and I nearly *died* laughing when she walked outside and put the hood on," Kaitlynn added smoothly.

"And? What happened?" Rob asked, hovering behind Palmer's chair.

"Well, the next day the girl had a crew cut and the hoodies were gone. For good," Ariana said with a conspiratorial smile. She would never forget how hard Noelle had laughed when she spied the girl's new coif. It was the beginning of their friendship.

"Anyway, from what I've heard, Martin Tsang is a member of some kind of . . . secret society?" Ariana said with a sly smile. Her fellow taps tensed up, realizing she was trying to talk about the societies without actually avowing knowledge of them. After all, Ariana still didn't know for sure who at the table was a member, and who was not.

"Right. He's in the Fellows," Palmer said, clearing his throat. "He's not the best at keeping it a secret."

"So, if the Fellows have robes . . . ," Kaitlynn said in a leading way.

"And what self-respecting secret society doesn't?" Jasper added.

"Then we could get not only Martin, but all of his friends, too," Ariana finished.

"They'd all have to get their hair cut," Palmer said, his eyes sparkling with mischief. "Do you realize what that means?" he said, looking at Lexa.

"That not only would we get them back, but we would find out who their members are. Every last one of them," Lexa said, giving Ariana and Kaitlynn an impressed look. "Not bad, girls," she said, taking a sip of her coffee.

Ariana hadn't even thought of that last angle, but she was glad Lexa had. This plan really *was* perfect.

"Lily, you're a genius," Maria said.

"Agreed," Conrad said with a smile. Kaitlynn beamed so brightly that Ariana was nearly blinded.

"And I just happen to know where the Fellows keep their supplies," Palmer whispered, leaning his forearms on his knees. "Last year at a crew party, Jeff Dorian got drunk and blabbed about it. They're in the back of the supply closets just off the Grand Hall."

"So let's do this!" Rob said loudly, clapping his meaty palms together.

"Now?" Lexa whispered, glancing over her shoulder at Martin and his pals.

"You're the one who said it has to be fast," Palmer said, getting up and grabbing his coat. "Let's go, you two."

Once again, everyone looked at Ariana and Kaitlynn.

"Us? Really?" Kaitlynn said, glancing at Conrad uncertainly.

Ariana was surprised as well. She would have thought the taps would be excluded from actual Stone and Grave business.

"Your brilliant idea. You're in," Palmer said, motioning for them to join him.

Ariana and Kaitlynn exchanged a giddy look. Ariana had just won major Stone and Grave points for both of them.

"Okay. But if we're coming, Jasper and Landon are coming too," Ariana said, feeling benevolent.

"Fine. The more the better," Palmer said. "Now let's do this."

Ariana, Kaitlynn, and the boys got up and gathered their things. As Ariana slipped past Lexa's chair, Lexa made no move to shift her legs out of the way.

"Are you guys coming?" Ariana asked Lexa and Maria.

"We told Soomie we'd meet her here after her grief counseling thing," Lexa said, waving a hand. "But I want to hear *all* the details."

Ariana glanced at Kaitlynn, who shrugged and tugged her coat on.

"Okay. We'll stop by your room later," Kaitlynn said.

Then she pulled Ariana away, following after the guys, who were already out the door.

"Why did you do that?" she whispered to Ariana as they hurried out.

"I want us both to get into Stone and Grave, Kaitlynn," Ariana replied.

Kaitlynn paused and narrowed her eyes. "Yeah?"

"Yeah," Ariana said, keeping her expression as frank as possible. "We're in this together now."

With a ponderous frown, Kaitlynn started walking again. Ariana fell into step with her and was surprised when Kaitlynn knocked elbows with her in a tentative but friendly way.

"Thanks, A," she said simply.

Ariana slipped her arm around Kaitlynn's, her heart thrumming over a job well done. "What are friends for?"

DARK SIDE

Ariana couldn't stop grinning as she sat against the cool wall in the grand hall, watching her plan come to fruition. She, Kaitlynn, Rob, Landon, and Jasper were all seated in a circle on the floor of the cavernous room, munching on gum and defiling the Fellows' royal blue velvet robes. Palmer was certain the Fellows would have a ritual tonight, though he wouldn't say why in all the secretiveness. But all they had to do was get the two dozen packs of gum chewed up before lights out. Ironically, all the chewing made them sound like a family of cows—which was kind of disgusting, but in a satisfying way.

"This is so gross," Kaitlynn said, tugging a wad of gum from her mouth between her thumb and forefinger. She placed it inside the royal blue hood on the velvet robe in her lap and grimaced.

"Yeah. I guess it wasn't so bad when it was just one piece of gum," Palmer replied, leaning past Ariana to better see her.

"Right," Kaitlynn said, her cheeks pink with pleasure. "At least with one piece you don't start to get lockjaw."

Palmer laughed as he tugged another of the robes toward him from the pile. "I can't believe this was your idea, Lily. Who knew you had a dark side?"

Ariana snorted a laugh and glanced at Kaitlynn. Her eyes clouded over for a moment, but then quickly cleared and she laughed as well. "Well, Ana was the one who realized it would work on the Fellows, so I guess we all have a dark side," Kaitlynn said.

Palmer looked at Ariana, his expression mischievous, and popped another piece of gum into his mouth. "I guess so."

Ariana felt warm all over, both from Palmer's leading tone and over the fact that Kaitlynn was throwing credit back at her.

"So, why do the Fellows use the grand hall for their rituals?" Ariana asked, glancing around at the expensive artwork that decorated the richly papered walls. "Isn't it kind of . . . out in the open?"

"Well, from what I've heard, the Fellows are dedicated to the memories of our founders, Atherton and Pryce," Palmer explained, using his thumbs to press his freshly chewed gum into the hood of a robe. "Because of that they have kind of a big ego as a group and feel like the two big guys are constantly looking over them or something."

Ariana wondered how he knew so much about the other society. Was it because he was president of Stone and Grave? Did people in power get to be privy to information like this somehow?

"That's lame," Kaitlynn said.

The guys laughed. "Seriously," Landon replied.

"Well, they're about to get their comeuppance," Jasper said, folding up the robe he'd just gummed.

"Comeuppance?" Ariana said with a smirk. "Who talks like that?"

"Seriously, dude. Join us in the twenty-first century," Rob joked, earning a hand slap from Landon.

"Thanks, *dude*. But I prefer to sound like an educated man, rather than an imbecile," Jasper shot back.

Rob's eyes flashed and everyone fell silent. Ariana exchanged a wary look with Kaitlynn. What was Jasper doing? Just the fact that Rob was there with them meant that he was probably a member of Stone and Grave. Was it wise for a plebe to cut him down that way?

"Whatever," Rob said finally, backing off.

Ariana let out a breath, but Jasper just went right on with what he was doing as if he hadn't noticed the moment of tension at all.

"All I know is, the barber in town is going to get a *lot* of business tomorrow," Palmer said with a laugh, popping a few more pieces of gum in his mouth. "Thanks to Ana."

Ariana felt Kaitlynn tense up next to her. Unbelievable. She had nothing to do with the idea, but already she felt so proprietary about it that she was offended over being left out.

"And Lily, of course," Palmer added graciously. The other boys whooped their appreciation.

Kaitlynn smiled. Ariana sighed in relief and allowed herself to bask in the attention. If she kept this up, she was going to get into Stone and Grave no problem. The future was hers.

And it felt good.

SHOO-INS

Ariana could not stop laughing. All around her, her fellow Privilege House denizens—and probable Stone and Gravers—were doubled over at the table, or trying desperately to keep their faces straight. But it was next to impossible. Every few minutes another student with half-chopped hair would walk by the table with his head ducked and a new wave of laughter would burst forth. The oddest thing was, it seemed as if every badly shorn student was, in fact, male, which meant the Fellows were all fellows.

"Omigod! Have you guys *seen* Martin Tsang?" Maria asked, slipping into a chair near the end of the table next to Ariana. "He looks like someone took a pair of garden shears to his head!"

"While blindfolded," Soomie added, cracking the first small smile Ariana had seen on her in days.

Ariana glanced over at Martin's table, giggling happily. He looked around and, finally unable to take the stares any longer, whipped out a gray skullcap and yanked it on over his hair. Ariana and her friends cracked up all over again.

"To Lily and Ana," Palmer said, lifting his glass of orange juice at the head of the table.

Ariana beamed across at Kaitlynn, who sat up a little straighter as the entire table full of students raised their glasses as well.

"To Lily and Ana!" they all chorused loudly, earning curious glances from students throughout the dining hall.

Ariana and Kaitlynn grinned as their friends swigged their juice and coffee in their honor. Tahira and Allison both shifted moodily in their seats, clearly annoyed at having been left out of the fun.

"Um, have I mentioned thank you?" Kaitlynn whispered, leaning across the table toward Ariana as she placed her juice glass down amid the many plates and bowls and cups.

"You don't have to thank me," Ariana replied happily.

Kaitlynn grinned back, and for the first time Ariana was truly certain that Kaitlynn was starting to believe in her friendship. She couldn't stop smiling as she speared a piece of scrambled egg with her fork and popped it into her mouth. Then, from the corner of her eye, she saw Palmer get up and walk around the table toward her. She glanced over at Lexa, her heart pounding, but for the moment Lexa was deep in conversation with Conrad and April.

"Hey, Ana," Palmer said, arriving at the end of the table. "Can I talk to you?"

Ariana felt Kaitlynn staring and her neck started to heat up. "Sure."

She pushed herself up from her chair, and she and Palmer shuffled over toward the wall.

"What're you doing?" Ariana whispered, glancing over her shoulder at their table.

"I just had to tell you . . . this whole prank thing has really upped your stock with the members," Palmer said, pride gleaming in his eyes.

Ariana's heart fluttered with excitement. "Wait, so are you telling me . . . ?"

Palmer grinned mischievously.

"You are. You're actually telling me straight-out that you're in—"

"Yes, I'm telling you straight out that I'm *in*," he replied flatly. "Which you already figured out, so really I'm not telling you anything you didn't already know."

Ariana pressed her lips together, overwhelmed with happiness that Palmer was trusting her with such a huge secret.

"After all this, you and Lily are practically shoo-ins," he told her, dropping his voice to a whisper as a couple of tweed-clad faculty members strolled by.

Ariana couldn't wait to tell Kaitlynn. "Really?"

"Really."

Palmer reached out and took her hand, holding it down by her side, where it was out of view of their table.

"Listen. I want to take you out somewhere," he whispered, his voice sending pleasant tingles down the backs of her legs. "Like on a real date."

Her eyes instinctively darted to Lexa. She and Conrad were whispering to one another, their heads bent close together. "Palmer—"

"I know. I know. You don't want to hurt Lexa," Palmer said. "But she's been going out with Connie for weeks already, and I'm getting tired of sneaking around."

"I kind of like the sneaking around," Ariana said.

Palmer grinned. "I like it too. But still. Don't you want to be able to do this"—he squeezed her hand—"without feeling like it's somehow wrong? Don't you want to be my actual girlfriend?"

Ariana's whole body responded to the question. "Of course I do. It's just . . ."

She glanced over at the table once more and this time her heart skipped a wild beat. Conrad had turned to talk to Christian, and Lexa was watching them, her eyes filled with anger. Ariana had never seen her look that way before. The second Lexa's gaze met Ariana's, she looked away, but the damage was done. Ariana slipped her hand out of Palmer's and took a step back. The fact remained that Ariana wanted—*needed*—to get into Stone and Grave, and Lexa was a member. Most likely a powerful member. If there was even the remotest chance that Lexa could block her membership, that she might blackball Ariana for the offense of going after Lexa's ex, then she had to be careful.

"Can I think about it?" she asked.

"Sure," Palmer said, standing up straight and taking a step back as well. He smoothed his APH tie. She could tell he was upset over being put off yet again. "Just don't keep me waiting too long."

As the tone sounded to end the breakfast period, Palmer smiled before loping off—which made Ariana feel better. He wouldn't have smiled if he'd been *too* upset. She took a deep breath to calm her nervous, excited heart, and walked back to the table to grab her coat and bag.

"What was that all about?" Kaitlynn asked suspiciously as Ariana pushed her arm into the sleeve of her leather jacket.

"Nothing," Ariana said. "He actually just wanted to congratulate us on the prank," she added quickly. "He said we're shoo-ins."

"Really," Kaitlynn said skeptically, narrowing her eyes. "Then why didn't he tell us both?"

"I don't know," Ariana said, lifting the strap of her bag onto her shoulder. "Maybe because he and I have been friends longer?"

"That's crap, Ana," Kaitlynn said as they walked away from the table. "There's something you're not telling me and we both know it."

"Lily," Ariana said. "There's not. I swear."

"Uh-huh," Kaitlynn replied, her expression sour as she looked Ariana up and down. "So much for all this talk about being friends."

Then she turned on her heel and stormed away. Ariana heaved a sigh and followed her toward the door, her giddy sense of victory all but evaporating. Sometimes dealing with a paranoid psychopath was hard work.

PRETENDING

"What was your best Halloween costume ever?" Maria asked, glancing over her shoulder at Ariana as they walked into the Hill with Lexa and Soomie that evening.

"I don't know . . . one year when I was little I dressed up as Fancy Nancy," Ariana said with a shrug.

"Like from the children's books?" Lexa exclaimed. "That's so cute! You should do that this year."

Ariana gave her a cautious smile. After the episode with Palmer in the dining hall that morning, she had expected the cold shoulder from Lexa. Had she somehow imagined Lexa's suspicion and jealousy? Would Lexa actually be fine if she found out about Ariana and Palmer's relationship?

"Um, I think we're a little old to be going as Fancy Nancy," Soomie said moodily, tugging her black scarf from around her neck as they crossed the room.

Ariana, Maria, and Lexa exchanged looks. Ariana knew that all of them were still sad, but while the others were trying to move on, act normal, cheer up, Soomie just couldn't seem to snap out of her depression.

"Right. Because Raggedy Ann is so much more sophisticated," Maria joked, clearly trying to keep the mood light as they joined the line at the coffee counter. The other girls fell in behind her. Every one of them knew that when it came to coffee, Maria went first.

"Whatever," Soomie sniffed, checking her BlackBerry.

Another look darted between Maria and Lexa.

"Last year Soomie and Brigit went as Raggedy Ann and Andy," Maria explained to Ariana. Soomie scoffed, like she didn't want to hear it. "What?" Maria pressed on. "It was hilarious with the big red noses and the red yarn wigs and the red-and-white striped tights."

"I only did that because it was Brigit's favorite toy as a kid," Soomie explained flatly. "This year was supposed to be my turn to pick a costume. We were going to be Batgirl and Robin. The costumes just came in the mail yesterday."

Ariana's stomach dropped. So that explained Soomie's new wave of melancholy.

"Well, at least you can still be Batgirl," Ariana suggested tentatively.

"You can't be serious," Soomie snapped. "You really think I'm going to wear that now?"

Ariana's throat prickled. "Sorry, I just—"

"Whatever," Soomie said, closing her eyes for a moment. She took a deep breath and looked Ariana in the eye. "*I'm* sorry. I just . . . I guess I'm not feeling very comic booky these days."

Ariana swallowed hard as the line inched forward. Maria looked down at her boots for a moment before flicking her long brown hair back and trying again.

"So . . . what're you going to be?" she asked Soomie.

"I don't know. I'm thinking something gothic," Soomie said.

"But Batgirl *is* gothic," Lexa said.

"No. I'm talking seriously gothic," Soomie said, ducking her chin. "Right now I've got it narrowed down to (A) Hester Prynne, (B) Jane Eyre, or (C) Joan of Arc."

Lexa looked at Ariana and whistled. "Yeah, I'd say that's gothic."

"Where is this party, anyway?" Ariana asked. "Did you rent out a club or something?"

"No. It's at my house," Soomie replied, sending a quick text on her BlackBerry.

"I thought your parents lived in California," Ariana said, her brow knitting. "Do they have a house in DC?"

"No. It's *her* house," Maria said with a grin.

Ariana blinked. "You have your own *house?*"

Soomie shrugged and slipped her PDA back into her bag. She looked up and narrowed her eyes at the chalkboard menu behind the coffee counter. "My parents know that I sometimes need my privacy, especially when I get stressed and need to concentrate. They want me to do my best here, so they bought it for me when I first started at APH. It's nothing big. Just a row house near the Capitol."

Ariana shook her head. Nothing big. She would have killed to have her own piece of real estate to retreat to. "That's incredible. I can't wait to see it," she said as they finally reached the counter.

"Can I help you ladies?" the guy behind the register asked with a smile.

Maria ordered her usual double espresso, then stepped aside so the rest of the girls could place their orders.

"I'll have a caramel latte and a pecan scone, please. Black coffee and a blueberry muffin for Soomie, and a regular latte and cinnamon scone for Ana," Lexa said, taking out her wallet.

"Oh, Lex, that's okay," Ariana said. "I got it."

"Please. You'll get the next one." She flipped her hair over her shoulder and eyed Ariana. "Maybe you should stick with the children's book theme. Go as Winnie the Pooh or Thomas the Train or something?"

"Okay, Lex. She's not a toddler," Soomie said.

Ariana smirked and scanned the room. Over at a table near the wall were three guys with seriously bad haircuts, which just made her smirk wider.

"Oh! What about Hannah Montana?" Maria said. "Or a Barbie doll?"

"Um, no," Ariana replied. "Why are you guys trying to saddle me with some juvenile costume?"

"Cuz it's fun," Lexa said with a half-shrug as the barista delivered their order.

"Ha ha," Ariana said to Lexa. "And thanks," she added, picking up her coffee and scone.

"Yeah, thanks, Lex," Soomie added.

Just then, Ariana caught a glimpse of Kaitlynn at the back of the line. Her face was buried in a book for English class and she was trying to look like she was oblivious to Ariana and the other girls, but Ariana knew better. Kaitlynn was wishing she was part of the conversation, and probably trying very hard not to horn in on it. Her usual style was to force herself on Lexa and the others every chance she got, but Ariana had a feeling that the whole Stone and Grave thing had Kaitlynn so freaked that she was rethinking her every move.

"Hey, Lily! Come join us!" Ariana shouted.

Kaitlynn looked up from her book as if startled. "Oh, I . . . I don't want to cut the line," she said.

"Sure you do," Lexa replied with a smile. "What do you want?"

Kaitlynn shrugged an apology at the waiting line of customers, but no one said a word. No one at APH ever contradicted Lexa Greene. "I'll just have a hot chocolate," Kaitlynn said.

Lexa ordered for her as Kaitlynn stood next to Ariana at the counter to wait. "So. What are you guys talking about?" she asked, tucking her book into her bag.

"Halloween costumes," Maria replied, sipping her espresso. "Ana can't decide what to be."

"I just hate pretending to be someone I'm not," Ariana said, shooting Kaitlynn a mischievous glance.

Kaitlynn hid a grin behind her hand.

"I have no idea what I'm going to be either," Kaitlynn said, taking her hot chocolate from the barista. Together the five girls turned toward the room and started the search for a big enough table to hold them.

"Why don't we do something together?" Ariana suggested.

"Really?" Kaitlynn asked.

"Sure. Why not?" Ariana replied, taking a sip of her coffee as she followed Lexa toward a table near the window. "It could be fun."

"You do realize that if we do a pairs costume you'll be stuck to my side all night," Kaitlynn said, lowering herself into a chair.

"I'm sure she can handle it," Maria said. "This is going to be fun! What's a good costume for Ana and Lily?"

"Tweedle Dee and Tweedle Dum?" Soomie suggested, her eyes innocently wide.

Ariana laughed, pleased that Soomie was actually making a joke, even if it was at her expense.

Lexa grinned. "I know! Dumb and Dumber!"

"You guys are hilarious," Ariana said acerbically, tearing a corner off her scone. "I was thinking more like Jane and Lizzie Bennet."

Kaitlynn gasped in excitement "Or the Boleyn girls!"

"But I want to be the one who doesn't get beheaded," Ariana replied.

"We'll see," Kaitlynn joked darkly, settling back in her chair and looking relaxed and happy. Still with the thinly veiled threats. But then, Ariana realized, she *had* set herself up for that one.

"This is going to be good," Ariana said with a smile.

"Definitely," Kaitlynn replied. "I'm so glad you decided not to cancel your party, Soomie. Suddenly I can't *wait* for Halloween."

GETTING TO KNOW YOU

"I must say, if this is what they call Hell Week, I'm unimpressed," Jasper said, reaching for a tortilla chip and dipping it into the salsa jar in the center of his dorm room floor.

"Why? Because they haven't made us do anything since Tuesday?" Ariana asked, flipping through her handbook. It contained basic information on her fellow pledges and on Conrad and April, the only two members who'd officially revealed themselves. It also covered the significance of various literary figures throughout history—like Lear and Miss Temple. Ariana had had it memorized since Wednesday morning, but tonight she'd finally taken Jasper up on his offer to study together. She wanted someone else to quiz her to make sure she hadn't missed anything.

"Exactly!" Jasper laid his book aside and rested his hands, palm up, on his knees. "I had all these visions of being up all night, toiling away at menial tasks, getting whipped by angry, faceless society members."

Ariana laughed and dusted some salt off her fingers. "Whipped?" Jasper raised his eyebrows. "I have a vivid imagination."

"Me too," Ariana replied. "But mine never went to whipping."

Jasper laughed and pulled his legs in closer, then reached for another chip. "So then, what did you think it was going to be like?"

With a sigh, Ariana leaned back against Jasper's roommate's bed. Kendrick Musgrove was out at a meeting of one of his "plethora of clubs," as Jasper put it, leaving the two of them some privacy to study. Ariana liked Jasper and Kendrick's room. It was neat and sparsely decorated. Both beds were covered in plain wool blankets. A few posters of Civil War battles and old-school navy ships lined the walls, hung at perfect right angles. She found the order comforting.

"I don't know. I suppose I thought it would be more like boot camp—you know, being woken up in the middle of the night and having to run around in our underwear or something."

Jasper laughed wholeheartedly, his white-blond bangs falling over his light blue eyes.

"Shut up," Ariana said, picking a few crumbs off her jeans to avoid his gaze. "My dad had to do that during fraternity pledging."

"Your dad was in a frat? Which one?"

Ariana froze as her vision entirely blurred over. Her dad *was* in a frat. *Her* dad. Not Briana Leigh's. She, in fact, had no idea whether or not David Covington had ever been in a fraternity. She didn't even know if the guy had gone to college. Her heart started to force hot panic through her veins and she could feel her throat begin to close. How could she be so careless? So stupid?

Breathe, Ariana. Just breathe.

In, one . . . two . . . three . . .

Out, one . . . two . . . three . . .

In, one . . . two . . . three . . .

Out, one . . . two . . . three . . .

It didn't matter. It wasn't as if Jasper was going to Google David Covington the second she left his room to try to find out what fraternity he was in. She looked up at him, her heart rate finally returning to normal. His expression was quizzical and slightly concerned.

"Sorry, I just . . . this is embarrassing, but I don't even know," she said with a laugh. "All that Sigma Delta Gamma stuff sounds the same to me."

"Believe me, I understand," Jasper replied. "Half the time when my dad starts talking my eyes just glaze over."

Ariana let out a silent sight of relief. "Anyhow, maybe they're taking it easy on us because of Brigit."

"Perhaps," Jasper mused, rubbing his hands together. He looked up at her, his blue eyes sparkling. "Or maybe it's all part of their insidious plan. Lull us into a sense of security so we'll be all the more surprised when they attack."

"Maybe."

"So," he said with a sly smile, reaching for his book again. He opened to a page at random and looked down his long nose at the small print. "Tell me everything there is to know about Adam Lazerri."

"Why bother? We both know it," Ariana said, tucking a strand of auburn hair behind her ear. "Poor Adam."

"Ah, yes. The sacrifice made for the greater good," Jasper said, toying with his book.

"Do you really think that's all it was?" Ariana asked. "That they were just trying to scare us into submission?"

Jasper shrugged and frowned. "Either that or they really are going to pick us off one by one."

"Well, I'm getting in, and so are you," Ariana said confidently. "So tell me all about yourself—things that aren't even in the handbook." She crossed her arms over her chest and settled in for the story.

Jasper smiled and let out a groaning sigh. He leaned back against his own bed, crooking both arms behind his head in a cocky way, and shoved his legs out, crossed at the ankles. "Well, where does one begin? There's so very much to tell."

"Start with the basics," Ariana said, rolling her eyes. "Then warm up to the good stuff."

"I grew up just outside Baton Rouge," Jasper replied, deepening his southern drawl. "Mama's family money comes from cotton, but Daddy's in the real estate biz. Although as far as I can tell he hasn't worked a day in his life. Just lived off the proceeds from investments made by his father's father."

"So what are you going to do?" Ariana asked. "Are you interested in real estate?"

Jasper pulled a face. "How could anyone be interested in real estate?" he said, faking a snore. He tugged at a pulled yarn in the throw rug beneath them. "No, I think I'll follow in my father's footsteps and do nothing."

Ariana laughed. "Right."

Jasper moved his hands to his lap where he folded them together. "Oh, I'm totally serious."

Ariana's brow knit. "What? No. How can you just aspire to do nothing?"

"Why not?" Jasper asked, lifting his shoulders. "The men and women of this country toil hard day and night to sock away enough cash so that they will one day, when they're old and gray, be able to retire and do nothing. I'd rather do nothing now. When I'm young. When I can really appreciate the blessing of being able to do nothing."

Ariana blinked a few times, trying to process this. She had never known anyone so unambitious in her life. All of her friends came from money, but they all aspired to something. Even if it was Kiran's dream to be a supermodel or Portia Ahronian's wish to marry an English royal. Everyone had to have something to look forward to. She looked at Jasper and saw what might have been a teasing glint in his eyes. Maybe he wasn't serious. Or maybe he was just enjoying the fact that his life's plan was throwing her.

"Well, congratulations. You're officially the lamest person I've ever met," Ariana said, only half-joking.

"I'm going to take that as a compliment," Jasper replied.

Suddenly, the door was flung open and in walked two guys in black hoods and ski masks. Ariana gasped.

"Oh, look," one of the intruders said. "Two for the price of one!"

Then he stepped forward and dropped a black bag over Ariana's head.

"Told you," Jasper said, his voice muffled. "Lulling us into a sense of security."

Ariana laughed through her hood.

"Shut it, plebe," the second attacker barked. "To the Tombs!"

Biting her tongue to keep from laughing, Ariana allowed herself to be manhandled out of the room.

DIFFICULT QUESTIONS

"Who are you?"

Ariana stared back at the masked and hooded Stone and Graver in front of her and pressed her lips together as a giggle threatened to escape. He was trying to be menacing, and yes, she was sweating like a pig under the hot interrogation lamps swinging overhead. And yes, the eyes of two dozen or more Stone and Grave members staring back at her from under their masks were making her dizzy. Not to mention the fact that her skin was on fire due to the torturously rough burlap bag she wore over her bare, perspiring skin. The problem was the question at hand. Her interrogator had no idea how difficult it was to answer.

She wasn't Ariana Osgood. Not anymore. But she wasn't exactly Briana Leigh Covington either. She wasn't the girl who grew up in Texas as an oil billionairess. She wasn't the girl whose mother died a long, slow death from cancer, and whose father was killed soon afterward. She wasn't the girl who had been drowned in Lake Page as collateral damage in a plan gone slightly awry.

Nor was she the girl who had drowned Briana Leigh. Not really. Yes, technically, the hands that had held Briana Leigh down under the water were the same ones that were now clenching the rope belt around her waist, but she was someone entirely different now. Someone who was ever evolving. The person who stood here now might be an entirely different person tomorrow.

"Who *are* you?!" the interrogator shouted again, getting right up in her face, so close she could hear him panting beneath his gruesome mask.

Next to her, Kaitlynn flinched and everyone in the Tombs held their breath. For a long moment, no one moved. A sudden and horrifying thought occurred to Ariana. Did they know? Was it possible that they had looked into Briana Leigh's background? Found pictures of her somehow? Realized that the Briana Leigh who had partied on South Padre Island last spring break was not the same person who was attending classes at Atherton-Pryce?

"Why do you deserve to be in Stone and Grave?" the masked figure demanded.

Ariana let out her breath. This was a much easier question to answer.

"Because I'm strong," she said calmly, her voice clear as day. "I'm a survivor."

The interrogator paused. Ariana liked to think he was surprised by her answer. Finally he let out a snort and stepped back.

"Oh, really? And what makes you such a survivor?"

Huh. Ariana wasn't sure how to answer that. She couldn't exactly tell him that she had broken out of a minimum security prison, gone on the lam for weeks on end, lied her way into Briana Leigh's life, and then killed the girl so that she could have a second chance at living.

Kaitlynn shifted next to her, the ragged sleeve of her sack dress scratching the bare skin just above Ariana's elbow. Suddenly Ariana knew exactly what to say, and Kaitlynn was *not* going to love it.

"Well, I'm not sure if you've all heard, but my father was murdered a few years ago," Ariana began, putting on a slightly haughty tone. After all, she had a feeling that no one else in this room had suffered through quite the level of tragedy that Briana Leigh Covington had. "By my best friend."

Ariana felt Kaitlynn stiffen, but she couldn't stop now. She was telling the truth. And no one but she and Kaitlynn knew that the murderer was standing in this very room.

"My mom had already died of cancer, so after that I was kind of on my own," Ariana continued, recounting Briana Leigh's life story. "I had to find a way to get over it and move on. But the whole thing not only made me stronger, it also made me realize that one day everything can be perfectly fine, and the next it can all be taken away like that." She lifted her right hand and snapped her fingers. "And it doesn't even have to make sense. It can just happen."

Ariana took a deep breath and folded her hands together at her waist.

"So now I live each day like it's my last. I appreciate everything more. My life, my friends, my family . . . what little I have left," she said in a mournful way. "But above all, I appreciate this opportunity. This brotherhood. And if I am given the honor of being initiated into Stone and Grave, you can be sure that I won't take the society, or my brothers and sisters, for granted."

There was a long moment of silence. Ariana could hear Kaitlynn breathing. The heat lamps above her hummed, and somewhere far off a door slammed. The interrogator turned his back on her and faced the membership of Stone and Grave. There was an almost imperceptible shift—Ariana couldn't even make out what it was—and then he turned around again.

"We deem your answer . . . acceptable," he said, bowing his head slightly.

And then he moved on to Kaitlynn. Ariana inflated with a rush of pride. It was all she could do to keep from glancing over at Jasper and grinning. He, Tahira, and Landon had already been deemed "acceptable." Ariana wished they could whip off their itchy robes and celebrate.

"Who are you?" the interrogator asked Kaitlynn.

"Lillian Oswald," Kaitlynn answered simply.

"That's it? Nothing to add?" he replied.

"It was a simple question," Kaitlynn said, lifting her chin.

He tilted his head in a menacing way. "Where do you come from? Who is your family? What do they do?"

Ariana's heart squeezed. These were simple questions, too, of course. Provided the person answering them had any sort of past to speak of. Ariana took the risk of glancing over at Kaitlynn. Much to her surprise, the girl appeared perfectly calm and collected.

"I'm not at liberty to say," she replied.

There was a distinct shift in the crowd of Stone and Gravers. They were clearly frustrated by Kaitlynn's answers. The interrogator's head tilted in the opposite direction.

"What do you mean, you're not at liberty to say?" If possible, his voice became even lower and more threatening.

Kaitlynn shrugged. "I'm not at liberty to say."

"Let me be sure I understand," the interrogator said, stepping closer to Kaitlynn. He held his hands, covered in black leather gloves, together in front of him. "You refuse to tell me where you grew up?"

"That is correct," Kaitlynn replied with a quick nod.

Ariana bit down on her tongue, hard.

"Who is your mother?" the interrogator demanded.

"I can't say."

"Your father?"

"I can't say."

The interrogator huffed. "Can't or won't?"

"Can't," Kaitlynn replied coolly.

The interrogator lifted his head. He crossed his arms over his chest. Ariana's pulse raced in her veins. What was she supposed to do here? She had promised Kaitlynn that she would help her get into Stone and Grave, but she was at a loss as to how to help her through *this*. There was no doubt in her mind that the membership would be pissed off if she spoke out of turn. And even if she could do that, what would she say? There was no way to defend Kaitlynn's refusal to answer their questions. What was she thinking?

The ominous silence continued. This was it. They were going to throw the history-free Lillian Oswald out on her ass. Ariana could feel it. She glanced over at Jasper and he was already looking at her—smirking—like, *Who does this girl think she is?*

Again, a very difficult question to answer.

Finally, the interrogator turned toward the membership. There was a flutter of sleeves. Something flashed in the dark. Ariana narrowed her eyes to try to see, but as quickly as she'd spotted it, it was gone.

The interrogator faced Kaitlynn again. Ariana held her breath.

"We appreciate your loyalty to family," he said, "and deem your answer acceptable."

Kaitlynn smiled. Ariana rocked back on her heels, shocked.

Crisis averted . . . for now, at least.

MADAME PRESIDENT

Allison's interrogation seemed to take an eternity. She recited her entire family line, the smirk on her face indicating that the brotherhood should be impressed by the number of dukes she was related to.

Ariana was so preoccupied with her own interrogation that she could barely focus on Allison's answers. The burlap felt as if it had developed a million tiny sets of teeth, all of which gnawed interminably at Ariana's skin. Sweat poured down her spine and sluiced along the backs of her bare legs. Her breath grew shallow. Any second she was going to rip the damn sack off and scream like she was on fire.

And then, finally, it was over. The interrogator turned to the group. Again the rustle. The flash. He turned around again and looked at Allison.

"We deem your answers . . . unacceptable."

Ariana's head snapped to the right. Allison's jaw dropped, her skin as white as snow.

"What?" Allison breathed.

"Kindly remove this one from the premises," the interrogator said, flicking a finger in Allison's direction.

Two masked figures swiftly dropped a black bag over Allison's head.

"What? No! What did I say? You can't just drag me out of here!" Allison shouted.

But drag her out they did. Tahira stepped out of line, her lips parted as if she was about to protest, but then Jasper grabbed her wrist and yanked her back before anyone could notice. Allison screamed and begged but didn't struggle as they shuffled her out. The whole thing was over in about five seconds. Allison was gone, and Ariana was left standing in line with only four others, shaking from head to toe. What had Allison said that was so horrible? Her answers had seemed rote and clinical, sure, but her lineage was impressive.

In the distance, there was a slam. And that was the end of Allison Rothaus's time with Stone and Grave. Mercifully, the heat lamps were flicked off. Ariana's skin cooled instantly, but just as suddenly she began to shiver in her own sweat.

Finally the interrogator slipped back into the crowd, disappearing among the other hoods, the other masks. Another figure emerged from the center of the group and everyone else quickly dropped down to their knees. Ariana looked frantically at Kaitlynn and Jasper. Were they supposed to bow too?

The figure paused before them. "I am Becky Sharp," she said. "I am the president of the APH chapter of Stone and Grave."

Ariana's heart was in her throat. She knew that voice. The girl reached up, slipped her hood from her dark brown hair, and removed her mask.

Lexa Greene stood before them, her skin ruddy from being trapped inside her mask.

"The rest of you have passed this trial," she said.

Ariana's mouth was dry. Lexa was president of Stone and Grave? *Lexa* was president? Sure, everyone at APH bowed down to her— figuratively at least—on a daily basis. But when Lexa had slipped and told Ariana about Stone and Grave, she'd acted as if she was scared. As if they would throw her out—or worse—if they found out she'd talked. Had it all been a lie? Had her admission really been a "slip"?

"As your reward, the membership will now reveal themselves." Lexa turned toward the group and raised her palms. "Brothers? Sisters? You may rise and remove your masks."

The group rose and Ariana felt an itch of irritation at the bold display of Lexa's power. But it was soon drowned out as the faces were revealed. Maria, Soomie, Palmer, Rob, and Christian all stood in a clump near the center of the group. Ariana's heart beat with excitement. She knew it. She knew all these people were in. But it was still elating to have her suspicions confirmed. The interrogator turned out to be Micah Granger—a gangly, doofy class-clown type whom Ariana never would have been intimidated by in real life.

"And now, for your next task," Lexa said with a wry smile.

She removed a stack of black envelopes from the belled sleeve of her robe and stepped forward.

"Well," she said with a short laugh. "We won't be needing this one." She frisbeed one of the envelopes at the pledges' feet, and Ariana saw the name *Allison* staring up at her in silver script. Tahira made a choking sound and covered her mouth. For a second Ariana stopped breathing, wondering if Lexa would react, but she simply ignored Tahira.

"Lillian," Lexa said, handing over an envelope.

"Briana Leigh," she said, meeting Ariana's eyes with a searching stare. Like she was trying to apologize or explain or, at the very least, gauge Ariana's reaction. Ariana took the envelope and looked past Lexa, hoping her feeling of betrayal wasn't evident on her face.

Lexa moved along, handing envelopes to Jasper, Tahira, and Landon. Landon immediately started to tear his open, but Lexa stopped him with a touch of her hand to his forearm.

"You must wait until you are alone," she said firmly. "And you are to share these tasks with *no one*. Not even with your fellow taps."

She stepped back to the center of the line and faced them once more.

"These tasks must be completed by midnight on Halloween if you wish to be considered for membership."

Right. Like anyone still here didn't wish to be considered for membership. If Ariana didn't want to be in Stone and Grave, she would have walked out when they made her strip down to her underwear upon arrival and then threw this awful burlap over her head.

"All right, then," Lexa said. She turned to her Stone and Grave brethren. "Let's send them on their merry way, shall we?"

The membership parted and two guys whom Ariana had seen milling around the Privilege House common rooms on occasion walked out from the back of the crowd. Their arms were laden with clothing—soaking wet, dripping piles of clothing—which they dropped at the pledges' feet with a loud *thwap*. Ariana looked down and instantly recognized her pink cashmere sweater at the top of the pile, two shades darker from being soaked in water. Her stomach twisted into a million humiliated knots. The membership had submerged their clothes. So now, after over an hour of torture to her skin, she was going to have to pull her soaking wet sweater and jeans on over her chaffed, chilled, sweat-caked skin and step out into the cold autumn night for heaven knew how long of a walk back to Privilege House.

Ariana was really starting to hate Stone and Grave. Even as she was dying to prove she was worthy of them.

"Well?" Lexa said, raising her eyebrows as the membership laughed. "Get dressed and go! You all have a *lot* of work to do."

THE TASK

"I can't believe they cut Allison," Tahira said as Ariana led the way up the long concrete steps of the tombs.

Behind them she heard the drip-drops of water coming off her fellow taps' clothing and the sucking sound of wet denim being pulled away from skin. She shivered violently and pulled the sleeve of her sweater past her hands to wring out some of the excess water. It sluiced down her arm all the way to her elbow, making the discomfort worse instead of better.

"I believe they were looking for something a bit more personal," Jasper said.

"Like Lillian gave them something more personal?" Tahira spat. "'I'm not at liberty to say. I can't say,'" she mocked, lowering her voice a few octaves. "She didn't say anything about herself, but somehow *that's* acceptable? This is so effing bogus!"

Kaitlynn gripped Ariana's arm from behind, clearly trying to bite back her frustration, and Ariana's toe hit the step in front of her. She tripped forward and nailed her head against something hard.

"Ow! God! Everyone just shut up a second!" Ariana blurted. Landon snorted a laugh and Ariana closed her eyes for a second, waiting for the throbbing in her forehead to pass. Then she took a deep breath and pressed her hand against the cold metal in front of her. Groping around in the darkness, her fingers eventually found a handle.

"Well. Let's find out where we've been all this time," she said, glancing over her shoulder before shoving the door open. Frigid air rushed in over her soaking wet body.

"Shit it's cold," Landon said, jumping up and down.

Ariana held her breath, wrapped her arms around her body, and pushed out into the night air. It took a moment for her eyes to adjust to the darkness. A thick fog had rolled across the grass, completely camouflaging the trunks of a line of trees so that they looked like nothing but a hovering tangle of branches floating over the earth. Ariana took a few steps away from the brick building and looked up.

The library. They'd just come out the back door of the library. So that explained the thousands of shelves of books that surrounded Stone and Grave's every ritual. The Tombs were actually the basement of the library—the place where old, obsolete books went to die.

"Wow. I could have sworn we were under the arts building," Landon said, his teeth chattering.

"Agreed," Jasper said. "Our kidnappers are clearly practiced in the art of misdirection. We're practically in the center of campus."

"You guys, do you realize what this means?" Ariana said.

Everyone turned to look at her, their feet disappearing beneath the fog, their breath mingling to create another cloud over their heads.

"What?" Kaitlynn asked.

Ariana's eyes shone. "They let us see where the Tombs are."

They all glanced at one another, letting the significance of this sink in.

"I don't get it," Landon said.

Ariana laughed. "We now know where their top secret meetings are held," she explained as she turned and started across the frost-bitten grass toward the hill. "They must be serious about letting the rest of us in."

"She's right," Jasper said, his chin up as they hurried along, one big, frozen group. "We must be getting close to initiation."

"Well, that's good," Landon said. "I'd be so pissed if I was randomly booted like . . . you know," he said, glancing guiltily at Tahira.

"I wish I had my cell," Tahira said. She looked up the hill toward Privilege House, where a few of the common room lights glowed through the darkness. "Allison must be freaking out."

"You don't need to call her. You'll be back inside your room in less than two minutes," Jasper pointed out.

"Yeah. If I don't freeze to death first," Tahira snapped back.

"I can't take this," Landon said. His lips were rapidly turning blue, and his shivering was growing more violent. "I say we run."

"Run?" Ariana asked, her molars clicking together.

"Faster you go, faster you get warm," Landon replied. "See ya!"

Then he turned and ran ahead, sprinting up the hill, his sneakers squishing with each step.

"Pop boy makes a good point," Tahira said. "Later." And she took off after him.

Ariana watched them go. After the emotional roller coaster of the last hour, she didn't have it in her to run.

"So, that was hilarious," Kaitlynn said under her breath.

"What?" Ariana asked as they came around the corner and onto the pathway that led to Privilege House. Jasper was lagging behind, strolling and whistling as if he didn't have a care in the world, as if the cold and wet didn't have any effect on him.

"The answer you gave them," Kaitlynn replied. "About Briana Leigh."

"I had to say something," Ariana replied, glancing sidelong at Kaitlynn. "Besides, I couldn't exactly answer how I wanted to, so I tried to think of how Briana Leigh might answer if she was actually here," she said quietly. "You know I'd never actually tell them the truth."

"I know," Kaitlynn said with a small smile. But her eyes were far away, and Ariana couldn't help feeling that she had undone some of the progress she'd made with Kaitlynn these past few days. There was a fine line between what might make her smile and what might send her into a murderous rage.

"So what was with all the 'I'm not at liberty to say' stuff?" Ariana whispered, glancing back at Jasper, who had fallen a few yards back and was still whistling a jaunty tune.

"Well, I figured they were going to ask about my past, so I decided that if they pressed it, I would tell them my parents are top secret diplomats and that I can't say anything more than that or I'll risk national security," Kaitlynn replied with a grin. "I mean, we *are* in DC and half the members have family in the government, so they'd probably understand."

"Not bad," Ariana conceded. In fact, she was impressed by Kaitlynn's creativity. But she also knew that national Stone and Grave had connections in *every* branch of government. If they really wanted to find out who Lillian Oswald's family was, they could. And if they tried, they would definitely find out that no one even remotely related to her worked in the government. There was no one related to her anywhere—she didn't even exist.

Of course she couldn't remind Kaitlynn of that. She had to be supportive of her friend. All she could do was hope that it never came to such an inquiry.

"Hi, ladies. Balmy night we're having, no?" Jasper said, finally falling into step with them.

"You're a little crazy, you know that?" Kaitlynn said to him.

"More than a little," he replied with a wide smile. "So, Ana . . . I was sorry to hear about your dad back there," he said, tucking his hands under his arms. "The same thing happened to my mom."

"Really?" Ariana and Kaitlynn said in unison.

Jasper blinked and lifted one shoulder as he walked. "Well, almost the same. I mean, she was shot, but she did it to herself."

He said it so matter-of-factly, Ariana's mouth dropped open in shock. "Wow. I'm . . . um . . . sorry."

Jasper shrugged again. "So . . . you going to open that?"

He nodded at Ariana's envelope, which she'd all but forgotten she had clutched in her hand.

"Now?" she said, looking down at the name *Briana Leigh* written across the front in silver script. "They told us to wait until we're alone."

Jasper smirked. "Do you always do as you're told?"

Kaitlynn let out a short laugh and Ariana's freezing cold face burned. If there was one thing she hated, it was being mocked to her face. But somehow, being mocked to her face in front of Kaitlynn was unbearable.

"Not always," she said flatly. "But in this case, yes."

With that she quickened her steps, walking purposefully ahead and leaving Kaitlynn and Jasper behind. She let the door of Privilege House slam behind her, not bothering to pay them the courtesy of holding it open, then bypassed the elevator, knowing they would only catch up with her if she waited. She jogged up the stairs and walked directly to the common bathroom at the center of her floor. No one ever used it because each dorm room had its own private bathroom. Even so, she waited until she was locked safely into the last stall before opening her envelope. She took a few deep breaths, waiting for her pulse to return to normal, then extracted the black card inside. Unfortunately, her breath left her all over again when she saw the task she'd been assigned.

"Catch Palmer Liriano in a compromising position."

For a long moment, Ariana couldn't move. *This* was her task? But *why*? Palmer was a member. Then an icy cold shiver of realization shot through her and she started to shake even more violently than before. Lexa. It had to be. She *did* suspect something was going on between Ariana and Palmer and this was her way of punishing Ariana for it. She was the president, after all. She would have the power to set the tasks. And now Ariana was totally screwed.

Ariana cursed under her breath and slammed her palm against the stall wall. Hell Week had officially earned its name.

BONDING TIME

"The assignment is not to directly translate the conversations into Spanish word for word, but to really think about colloquialisms and slang," Mr. Bernal instructed, pacing the front of the classroom. His wiry black hair stuck out in all directions and stubble peppered his double chin. Sometimes it was all Ariana could do to keep from gagging when he walked into a room. She just could not understand people who didn't bother to take pride in their appearance. "Word-for-word translations often wind up sounding too formal, and descriptive words sometimes have a more exact version in the Spanish, so you'll really need to dig into your vocabularies."

Mr. Bernal snorted some phlegm. Ariana cringed and averted her gaze, staring down at the cursor on the screen of her laptop, watching its blink, blink, blink. She sighed and waited for the teacher to say something she actually needed to type.

"To make it a bit easier on you, I've decided to have you work on this in pairs," Mr. Bernal continued.

Ariana automatically glanced at Lexa, who was sitting one row over, next to the window. Lexa grinned and Ariana smiled back, but her heart felt tight in her chest. All day on Sunday Ariana had avoided Lexa, trying to figure out how exactly she was supposed to act around her now. If Lexa had set her Stone and Grave task, then clearly she knew something was going on between Ariana and Palmer. But *how much* did she know? Was Ariana supposed to talk to her about it or play dumb?

The real question was, who was going to mention it first? And if Ariana did, would that make her look weak or strong in front of Lexa—the person who was supposed to be her good friend, the person who was the president of the secret society she wanted to get into more than anything?

The class-ending tone sounded, and everyone started to gather their things. Ariana snapped her laptop closed and slipped it into her bag. Lexa lifted the strap of her messenger bag over her shoulder and fell into step with Ariana on their way out the door.

"Want to get together later and figure out which scene we want to translate?" Lexa asked. The red turtleneck she was wearing brought out the rose color in her cheeks, and her eyes were bright and happy, like everything was perfectly normal and there was no Palmer-shaped elephant between them.

"Sure," Ariana replied, holding the door open for Lexa as they stepped into the bustling hallway. They sidestepped a freshman couple who were lip-locked next to the water fountain and headed for the stairs.

"So. Aren't you going to ask me how brunch with my parents went yesterday?" Lexa asked.

Ariana's heart skipped a snagged beat. She'd completely spaced on Lexa's state-of-the-union chat with her parents.

"Sorry. Right. How was it?" she asked.

"Stupid," Lexa replied, gazing straight ahead. "They were all formal with each other. Nobody talked about anything real. They only did it so that the photogs could get shots of the three of us together. My dad even told a lame joke as we came down the steps of the restaurant, just so they'd get all of us smiling. It's all so fake."

"So did you?" Ariana asked.

Lexa's brow knit. "What?"

"Smile," Ariana said.

Lexa paused in front of the bathroom door near the end of the hall. "Of course," she said. Like the question of whether or not she was going to help keep up her parents' ruse wasn't even a question at all. "Hang on. I need to make a gloss stop," she said, shoving open the bathroom door.

As Ariana entered the bathroom, Lexa bent down to check under the doors of the two stalls, making sure they were alone. Ariana's heart started to pound. This was it. Lexa was going to ask her about Palmer. The elephant pressed its massive foot down on her chest, making it impossible to breathe.

"I have a question for you," Lexa said, dropping her bag on the counter next to one of the sinks. Ariana braced herself. "About Lillian."

Ariana blinked but didn't relax. Instead, her pulse started racing in a completely different direction. Lexa dug through the outside pocket of her bag and came out with a tube of berry-colored gloss.

"Okay," Ariana said warily. She joined Lexa at the sinks, leaning her hip against the counter.

"Does she ever say anything about her family?" Lexa asked, dabbing some gloss on her lower lip. "Any brothers or sisters? Anything about going home for the holidays?"

Ariana swallowed hard. "Not really."

"Huh. It's odd, isn't it?" Lexa said, taking out her eyeliner. "I mean, she's so friendly and talkative most of the time. You'd think she'd be one of those people who never shut up about their friends and family."

"Well, we're not really that close," Ariana replied.

Lexa blinked. "But she told you all those stories about her old school. About pranking that girl and everything. Do you know where she used to go?"

Ariana turned to the sink and turned it on full blast. Son of a bitch. Of course that story made it sound like she and Kaitlynn were best friends, up all night talking and bonding and reminiscing.

"No. I don't think she ever mentioned the name of the school," she said, reaching for the soap.

"Weird," Lexa said, capping the eyeliner. "We checked with admissions, and even they don't have a copy of her most recent transcripts. How did she even get in here?"

"I don't know, but they must have reviewed her file," Ariana said, scrubbing her hands hard to mask the fact that they were trembling.

"This school's next to impossible to get into. They don't take just anyone, right?"

"True," Lexa said. She looked at her reflection and smoothed the hem of her long shirt over her hips.

"Maybe there's a reason it all needs to be kept a secret," Ariana suggested. "Maybe she's in the witness protection program or something."

Lexa paused in her grooming, arching one eyebrow. "Huh. Interesting."

Ariana shut the water off and turned to grab a paper towel, her nerves quivering. She had to change the subject and she had to do it fast. She decided it was time to bite the bullet. If Lexa wasn't going to mention the elephant, she would. Maybe it would stop her from feeling so tense, give her the power in this conversation, if she showed Lexa that she wasn't going to be cowed by her games.

"I have a question for you, too," Ariana said. "About the tasks."

Was it her imagination, or had Lexa just flinched? Was talking about the tasks outside the Tombs verboten?

"Okay," Lexa said, crossing her arms over her chest.

"Well, what if the task is kind of subjective?" Ariana asked, turning to face Lexa again. "Like my last one—I was supposed to make a spectacle of myself, but I wasn't sure how big of a spectacle was required."

This was true. When Ariana had first received her task she had been clueless as to what to do and therefore terrified of getting it wrong. But in the end, she had been pretty proud of herself for her performance. She had walked into the dining hall right in the middle of a meal, climbed up on a table, and performed a song and dance for everyone to see. She still smiled every time she thought about the resulting standing ovation.

Lexa laughed and lifted her bag strap over her head again. "Well, you executed that one perfectly. I'm sure you'll do fine."

Ariana eyed Lexa. She had assumed that the task was her friend's way of punishing Ariana and Palmer for getting together. But there was no teasing lilt in Lexa's expression as they stood together in the bathroom. No knowing glances. So maybe Ariana was just being paranoid. Maybe it was April and Conrad's job to come up with the tasks. Could one of *them* suspect Palmer and Ariana? Was Conrad trying to get revenge on his new girlfriend's ex?

Thinking about it all made Ariana's head hurt.

"Well, I'm glad *you* think so," Ariana said.

"Whatever you do, just make sure you get it done by the deadline," Lexa advised curtly.

"Of course," Ariana replied, stung.

"I'm just trying to help." Lexa crossed her arms over her chest. "You don't want to know what'll happen if you fail. Believe me."

Ariana felt as if she'd just been slapped. Where did Lexa get off talking down to her like that? She'd never copped an attitude with Ariana before. Did she think that it was okay to do so now that Ariana knew Lexa had power over her? All this time Ariana had been tiptoeing around the girl, keeping her relationship with Palmer on the back burner just to spare Lexa's feelings. And to keep herself in the running for Stone and Grave as well, but still. It had started out as an attempt to spare Lexa's feelings. But clearly, Lexa didn't care quite as much about sparing Ariana's.

"Come on. We're gonna be late for English," Lexa said, brushing past Ariana and yanking open the door.

"I'm right behind you," Ariana said.

The second the door swung shut behind Lexa, Ariana whipped out her cell phone and sent Palmer a text.

RE: YOUR INVITE. I'M IN.

CHEESY

"I have to confess, when you said you wanted to take me out on a real date, I thought there would probably be a restaurant involved," Ariana said as she tucked her coat underneath her legs and settled down on the cool marble steps in front of the Lincoln Memorial. All around them, tourists paused to take pictures and security guards strolled back and forth along the foot of the stairs. A group of laughing schoolchildren chased each other up the steps, shouting to each other in a foreign language.

"Well, this is my favorite spot in the city," Palmer confided, dropping down next to her. "I mean, check out this view," he said, lifting a hand toward the Washington Monument and the Reflecting Pool in front of it. He wore a gray wool coat over his black turtleneck, and his black hair fell over his forehead. He was so handsome, Ariana felt warm just looking at him.

Ariana took a deep breath of the crisp fall air and tore her gaze reluctantly from Palmer. The sun was just starting to dip behind the monument, and the beautiful colors of the sunset were reflected in the water of the long, rectangular pool.

"Okay. I'll give it to you," Ariana said. "It *is* beautiful here."

"Besides, I packed a picnic basket," Palmer pointed out, lifting an old-school wicker basket onto the step between them. "That's kinda romantic, right?"

"Depends on what you've got in there," Ariana joked, angling her chin to try to see inside.

Palmer extracted two linen napkins, one of which he flicked open and lay across Ariana's lap. Then he did the same with his own. He reached into the basket again and came out with two covered bowls and two spoons.

"It's a famous family recipe and one of my favorite things to eat in the fall," he said, handing her a bowl and spoon. "Veal stew."

Ariana peeled the lid off her bowl, and steam wafted from the scrumptious-smelling dish. She could see bits of peeled potato and carrot and onion nestled in among the morsels of meat.

"How did you make this?" she asked. "Does Alpha tower have a gourmet kitchen I don't know about?"

"I didn't actually make it myself," Palmer confessed sheepishly. He took out two water bottles, popped their tops, and handed one to her. "I called home and had my mom's cook whip it up and drive it over. But if I had a kitchen at my disposal, I absolutely would have cooked it myself. I'm an excellent chef."

"Really?" Ariana asked with a smile.

"You should try my peanut butter and jelly and Eggo waffle sandwiches," Palmer said seriously. "I've had several restaurateurs offer to buy the recipe from me, but I refuse to sell out."

Ariana laughed and took a bite of her stew. The meat practically melted in her mouth.

"Palmer, this is amazing," she said as he placed a basket of crusty bread down on the step behind them. "Thank you so much for sharing your secret family dish with me."

"Of course," Palmer said with a grin. He stirred his stew with a spoon, blushing and smiling as he looked down into the bowl. "There are a lot of things I want to share with you, Ana."

Ariana's heart flipped and she glanced over at him. He met her eye and laughed.

"That was insanely cheesy, wasn't it?" he asked.

"Kind of," she said, scrunching her nose. Then she laughed as well and reached over the basket to touch his arm as his blush deepened. "No! I'm just kidding! It was sweet."

"I'm just saying. . . ." Palmer shrugged and turned his knees toward hers on the steps. "I want to do more stuff like this with you. Sometimes I spend whole class periods just thinking about all the places we can go together and all the things we can do."

"Really? Which class periods?" Ariana asked with a grin.

"Chemistry, mostly. God, I hate chemistry," Palmer said.

"Me too," Ariana replied.

"To hating chemistry, then," Palmer said, lifting his plastic water bottle.

"Except ours," Ariana replied, clicking her bottle's neck against his.

Palmer looked at her, his bottle frozen halfway to his mouth. "Now *that* was cheesy."

Ariana giggled. "I guess we just bring it out in each other."

Palmer smiled a smile that sent Ariana's heart fluttering around like a butterfly. "Yeah. I guess we do."

Leaning slightly into his side, Ariana sighed contentedly. She was glad she had said yes to Palmer's invitation. If Lexa's plan had been to drive her and Palmer apart, it clearly wasn't working. In fact, it had the exact opposite effect. She half-wished Lexa would walk by so Ariana could wave and say something coy like, "Hey, Lexa. Have you met my boyfriend, Palmer?" just to show her how her little task was not getting to her.

But for now, this was enough. Because for the moment, Ariana felt more in control of the situation than ever. Which was just the way she liked it.

NO NOELLE

"So, Landon's at the library cramming for some English exam with his study group," Palmer said, squeezing Ariana's hand as they walked through the hushed lobby of Privilege House after their date. Ariana could hear a few of the cardio machines humming in the gym and the TV playing at a low volume in the lounge, but otherwise the place was quiet. "Want to come up?"

Ariana felt his invitation in every inch of her body. There was nothing she wanted more than to come up. But ever-so-suddenly her skin stopped tingling. Because she immediately thought of the camera she'd put in her purse before the date and started to wonder whether she could position it in such a way that it could record what was happening between them. Started pondering how she could hide it from Palmer and get the best angle. Realized that by tonight, her Stone and Grave task could be complete—if only she was willing to sully the perfect evening she and Palmer had spent together.

And then she started to feel nauseated.

"Ana?" he asked, raising his eyebrows.

"Actually, I don't think that's the best idea," she said.

The boys' elevator pinged and a couple of sophomore guys walked out, gabbing about their high scores on some video game. Palmer automatically dropped Ariana's hand, but the guys didn't even seem to notice them there. She expected him to reach for her fingers again once they were gone, but he only stepped further away.

"Not the best idea, huh?" he asked, shoving his hands into the pockets of his wool coat. "Did I do something? Or is this about Lexa again?"

Ariana swallowed a lump that had formed in her throat.

"No. It's not about Lexa, I swear," she said, stepping toward him. "Honestly, I just . . . I think I probably shouldn't have had that ice cream on top of the stew."

Palmer's handsome face instantly creased with concern. He reached up and touched her cheek, tucking a stray lock of auburn hair behind her ear. "I'm sorry. You don't feel well? You should have said something."

"And make my new boyfriend aware of my weak stomach?" Ariana joked, tears stinging her eyes over the ruined romance of the night. Two seconds ago Palmer had been thinking about kissing her. Now he was probably thinking about watching her throw up. "Not likely."

Palmer gave her a small smile. "Do you want me to walk you back to your room?"

"No, thanks. I'll be okay," Ariana said.

"Okay. Well, text me if you need anything."

He reached over and hit the up button on the girls' elevator, then leaned down and kissed her forehead. Great. Thanks to the specter of her stupid Stone and Grave task hanging over her head, she wasn't even going to get a proper kiss good night. A perfectly romantic first date had just been ruined by some Stone and Graver's idea of a joke. When one day she found out who actually did write the tasks, she was going to smack that person upside the head.

The elevator pinged and the doors slipped open. Ariana stepped inside and gave Palmer an awkward wave. The second the doors closed again, she rested her forehead against the cold metal surface in front of her and groaned in frustration.

How was she ever going to complete the task of catching Palmer in a compromising position? She cared about the guy. Not only that, she didn't want to cheapen their new relationship by recording their time alone together. It made the very idea of kissing him, of being with him, feel sleazy. What kind of task was this? Ariana wished she could find out what directives the other taps had been saddled with. Were all the tasks this awful? This personal?

She shoved open the door to her dorm room and Kaitlynn instantly popped up from her bed, dropped the book she was reading, and plucked out her ear buds. She was wearing pink striped pajama pants with a matching cropped tank top and had her short hair pushed back from her face with a white headband.

"You went out on a date with Palmer Liriano!" she hissed, shoving an accusing finger toward Ariana's face. "I knew it! I knew something was going on with you two!"

Ariana's heart sank as she shrugged off her coat. "What'd you do? Follow me?"

"Only to the door. I saw him pick you up and you both looked very giddy," Kaitlynn said, crossing her arms over her chest. "Was that his car, by the way? Because . . . suh-weet!" she sang.

Ariana rolled her eyes. Yes, the Audi convertible Palmer kept in the garage on campus was rather lush, but it was pretty much the last thing on her mind at the moment.

"Fine. Forget the car. Why didn't you tell me?" Kaitlynn demanded.

"I'm trying to keep it a secret," Ariana replied, turning to hang her coat in her closet. "I don't want anyone to know yet."

"You mean you don't want Lexa to know," Kaitlynn said, lifting one eyebrow. "Because if your BFF found out you were dating her ex-bf she might try to keep you out of Stone and Grave. Which she could definitely do considering she's the president."

Got it in one.

"Is this where you threaten to tell her?" Ariana asked, sinking down onto her bed, suddenly exhausted. "Because I'm kind of exhausted, so if we could save that part for the morning . . ."

"No," Kaitlynn said. "Why would I do that? I thought we were supposed to be friends."

Ariana perked up slightly. No threats? Really? "True," she said.

"So, friend," Kaitlynn said, bouncing down onto the bed next to Ariana and slinging her arm over her shoulders. "Tell me *all* about your date! Where did he take you? What did you do? Did you two hook up or what?"

Ariana took a deep breath, knowing that she was going to have to spill. But suddenly she felt melancholy and nostalgic. Nostalgic for Noelle Lange, her former roommate and best friend at Easton Academy. If Noelle were here, Ariana would tell her all about the awkward way in which the date had ended. Would ask for her advice about what to do next. How to make it all go away. And Noelle would know what to do. She always knew.

"Well, he took me to his favorite place in DC," Ariana began, folding her legs under her story-style and turning to face Kaitlynn on the bed. "The steps of the Lincoln Memorial."

Kaitlynn's face fell. "Really? Connected millionaire boy took you to a free tourist attraction?"

Ariana tried not to grimace. Leave it to Kaitlynn to disparage the best part of the night. "No! It was romantic, really."

Then she sat back in her hands and gushed all about the picnic and the sunset and the conversation, feeling dirty all the while. These were the kind of details that should have been saved for a real best friend, not wasted on Kaitlynn Nottingham.

But it was all for the greater good. Every moment with Kaitlynn had its purpose. And sooner or later, even this would prove to be worth it.

I NEVER

"The whole point of the I Never task is for you to get to know each other better," Conrad said, placing a full bottle of vodka on the floor in front of each of the taps. "So be creative."

Ariana looked around the circle at the other four taps on Wednesday night. They were once again wearing their itchy burlap robes, and they were seated on the cold concrete floor of the Tombs, their thighs bare against the hard, frigid surface. Ariana eyed the bottle of vodka with apprehension and revulsion. Losing control had never been her favorite thing, so she'd never been a big drinker. Back at Easton, when her friends had gotten together the occasional game of I Never, she had almost always cheated and lied, claiming not to have done things she had, in fact, done. Like the time Taylor Bell had said she'd never broken into a faculty member's room, and Ariana hadn't taken a drink, even though she *had* done that before—with Thomas Pearson. But she couldn't share that story with her friends. They had never even known that she and Thomas were friendly, let alone breaking-and-entering-together friendly.

But lying to Stone and Grave was a whole other level of complicated, because she was supposed to be Briana Leigh, and she had no idea what Briana Leigh had never done. What if they *knew* the things Briana Leigh had and hadn't done—Lexa *had* gone to camp with Briana Leigh—and she got it wrong?

Suddenly, Ariana's underarms started to prickle. A sensation she detested almost as much as the foggy, light-headed feeling she got from drinking too much.

"The rules, just so we're clear, are simple," Conrad explained. "When it's your turn, you are to tell us something you've never done. Anyone in the circle who *has* done this thing is to take a drink. If you haven't, you can leave your bottle on the floor in front of you. That's it. So. Who will volunteer to start?" Conrad asked, stepping back and crossing his arms over his broad chest.

"I'll go, Brother Lear," Jasper said, lifting a finger as if he was summoning a waiter.

"Thank you, tap," Conrad said. He stepped back toward the group of brothers and sisters, standing between Lexa and April, both of whom grinned giddily. "Go ahead."

Ariana felt a shift in the crowd around her, a shimmer of excited anticipation, and she felt a sour burning in her chest. This wasn't about them getting to know each other better. They were playing this game for the entertainment of the membership. Hazing at its finest.

"I never kissed a guy," Jasper said with a smirk.

Tahira rolled her eyes, opened her bottle, and took a swig. Kaitlynn did the same. Ariana touched the bottle to her lips and tried not to wince as the alcohol burned its way down her throat. Then Landon grabbed his bottle and took a drink. A few people in the crowd laughed and whispered.

"What?" he said, drawing the back of his arm across his glistening lips. "I'm a rock star."

"Try pop star," Rob corrected, standing on his toes to be seen. His comment earned another round of derisive laughter. Landon blushed but smiled. The guys often ribbed him about his pretty-boy pop persona, but he never seemed to mind. Probably because that pretty-boy pop persona had already netted him millions and taken him around the world, where he'd played sold-out concerts and met hordes of screaming, worshipping fans.

"Next?" Conrad intoned, looking down his nose at Ariana.

Ariana took a deep breath. It was her turn. Which meant, at least, she wouldn't have to drink this time. "Okay. *I've* never kissed a girl," she said.

Everyone except Kaitlynn drank. All eyes went to Tahira.

"What?" she said in the exact same tone as Landon. "I'm a slut."

Everyone laughed and Ariana's shoulders started to relax. At least no one was taking this all that seriously. Games of I Never with Noelle Lange and Gage Coolidge were seriously stressful, since they both seemed to know everyone's secrets and took pride in outing them. Not that Ariana hadn't come up with a few fabulous I Nevers in her day, perfectly crafted to humiliate or expose her friends. But the stakes in this game were much higher, and laying low seemed the better tack.

Tahira was up next. She leaned back on her hands and looked right at Ariana. Ariana's eyes narrowed and all the tiny hairs on the back of her neck stood on end. What was the girl up to?

"I've never stolen anything . . . ," she said in a leading way.

Ariana stopped breathing. She wasn't. She couldn't. Was she really going to try to call out Ariana for those thefts she'd committed at the beginning of the year? Her eyes darted around at the membership, finding Christian in the crowd, thinking of his Rolex, which she'd lifted from the boathouse that day during welcome week. Oh God. They were definitely going to ask for an explanation and then she'd have to come up with some kind of cover story on the fly. But what? How could she, millionaire orphan Briana Leigh Covington, explain stealing thousands of dollars worth of jewelry and iPods and random paraphernalia from her classmates? Ariana's stomach twisted dangerously and her vision started to prickle over with gray spots. This was all Kaitlynn's fault. If Kaitlynn hadn't blackmailed her, she wouldn't have had to steal those things.

". . . from the school bookstore," Tahira finished finally.

Ariana released her breath. She looked at Tahira, her face burning. Tahira grinned back. She'd done her damage and she knew it. It was all Ariana could do to keep from slapping the little twit across the face. Meanwhile, both Landon and Jasper reached for their bottles.

Breathe, Ariana. Just breathe.

In, one . . . two . . . three . . .

Out, one . . . two . . . three . . .

In, one . . . two . . . three . . .

Out, one . . . two . . . three . . .

"Theft, huh?" Conrad said, eyeing Landon and Jasper from above. "Care to explain?"

"I forgot my wallet and I was out of gel," Landon said matter-of-factly.

The guys jeered and hooted and hollered. Landon simply shrugged. "Dude's gotta do what a dude's gotta do."

Conrad looked at Jasper. "And you?"

"It was a freshman dare," Jasper replied. "My friends said I couldn't walk out of there with a pencil. I took a laptop."

Silence reigned. For a moment Ariana was concerned for Jasper's future with Stone and Grave, but Conrad actually looked impressed.

"All right then," he said. Then he turned to Kaitlynn, his soft black robe swishing. Ariana could have reached out and touched that cozy-looking velvet. She yearned to tear the burlap sack from her sweaty, raw skin and slip one of those luxurious robes on instead.

One day, she told herself. *One day soon.*

"Next?" Conrad said.

Kaitlynn smirked as her gaze flicked to Ariana. A hot flush raced over Ariana's already warm body. She tried to breathe normally, but she was starting to hyperventilate. Now what?

"I've never killed anyone," Kaitlynn said, her voice loud and clear.

The membership laughed and scoffed and whispered as Ariana's insides plummeted to her toes. First of all, Kaitlynn was lying. She had murdered Briana Leigh's father in cold blood. Second, did she really think Ariana was going to take a drink? No. No way. She just wanted to get a rise out of her. This was payback for what she'd said during the interrogation the night Allison had gotten kicked out. Then Ariana saw something move to her right. Jasper was reaching for his bottle. Suddenly, everyone froze. The Tombs were silent. Jasper took a long drink from the bottle. Then, ever so innocently, he looked around at the membership.

"Lucy. She was my dog," he said. "I had her put to sleep when the cancer spread to her lungs."

Relieved laughter filled the room. Ariana rolled her eyes and smiled. For a second there she really thought there was another murderer in their midst. Jasper placed his bottle down on the concrete with a ping and everyone looked at Landon expectantly. What exactly could superstar Landon Jacobs claim to have never done?

"I've never *not* completed my task for Stone and Grave," he said with a Cheshire smile.

Never not, Ariana thought. *That means he's already done it. And I should drink because I haven't.* She reached for her bottle, but paused when she realized no one else had made a move. Suddenly, all eyes were on her and her hovering hand. Ariana's heart pounded wildly. Was she really the only tap who hadn't completed her task? But they'd just been given their envelopes on Saturday, and they still had a week and a half to get them done. This was not good. The last thing she wanted was for the membership to know she was the only one whose task wasn't completed. They were going to think she wasn't dedicated to earning her membership.

But it was already too late. They'd all seen her reaching for her bottle. The only thing to do now was bite the bullet.

Ariana grabbed her bottle and took a drink. She saw several of the members exchange interested and impatient glances, and she dared not look at Lexa. She braced herself for the inevitable question from Conrad.

"I've never been on a roller coaster," Jasper said suddenly, cutting the tension.

"What? Seriously? That's sick!" Landon said, grabbing his bottle.

"God did not intend us to hang upside down at ninety miles an hour. If he had, he would have given all of us wings," Jasper said.

The membership started to tease and needle Jasper while Tahira, Ariana, and Kaitlynn all drank. Just like that, the tense moment with Ariana in the spotlight had passed. As Ariana lowered her bottle she glanced at Jasper in thanks. He smiled back. He'd distracted the members on purpose, just to save her. She wouldn't have been surprised if his admission were a lie. A lie told just to help her out.

But still, an awful, heavy feeling of failure and dread settled in over her shoulders. All the other taps had completed their tasks, and she hadn't even come up with a plan to execute hers. She'd been hoping for a miracle—for some kind of reprieve. But now it was clear that reprieve wasn't going to come. And if she wanted to measure up to her fellow taps, she was not only going to have to complete her task, but she was going to have to do it soon.

Ariana's eyes found Palmer in the crowd, and he gave her a private smile of encouragement for her turn. Her heart thumped painfully as she wondered if, after she finished her task, he would ever smile at her like that again.

THE POWER

Ariana lay back on her bed, her heart pounding bile through her veins. She breathed in through her nose and out through her mouth, counting slowly to ten. Then she pushed herself up and slipped her phone out from behind the seasonal mum atop her dresser. She had bought the potted flower that afternoon at the APH bookshop, which was chock-full of autumnal decorations these days, but she hadn't felt very festive doing so. Her fingers trembling, she stopped the recording and quickly played it back.

There she was, staring at the camera, the picture so clear she could see her ice-blue eyes. She should have felt gratified. This was going to work. But she hated that it was going to work.

Taking another deep breath, Ariana erased the ten-second video to make more room on the digital card. She carefully replaced the phone in its hiding spot, then sat down on her bed to wait, kneading her fingers in her lap.

You have to do this. There's no other way. If you want to be in Stone and Grave, you must complete this task.

An image of Lexa's smirking face flashed through her mind and Ariana's fingers curled so quickly, her nails cut into her palms. The very idea that she was going to do this to Palmer just because of some sadistic vendetta Lexa had against her made her blood boil. Palmer and Lexa had broken up weeks ago. And Lexa had a new amazing boyfriend. Why couldn't she just let Palmer go? Was she trying to make sure he never dated again?

Calm down. It wasn't necessarily her, Ariana reminded herself. April was always a possibility. She was the girls' pledge educator. She was supposed to be in charge of Hell Week, along with Conrad. It might have been her job to figure out what each of the girls would have to do. But if so, what was she thinking, making one of the taps humiliate one of the active members?

It was Lexa. It had to be Lexa. Ariana knew she was just fooling herself thinking otherwise.

There was a quick rap on the door and Ariana's breath caught. She closed her eyes, took a breath, and held it. In a few minutes this would all be over.

Just breathe, Ariana.

In, one . . . two . . . three . . .

Out, one . . . two . . . three . . .

She opened her eyes, reached over, and hit the record button on her phone. Her hands were perfectly still. She got up, walked to the door, and opened it. Palmer was wearing a blue APH sweatshirt and his eyes were bright.

"I got your note," he said, holding up the scrap of paper between two fingers. "'Let's make up for the other night?'"

Ariana opened her mouth to greet him, but her airway was choked off by guilt. So instead she grabbed him by the front of his sweatshirt, the embroidered letters crushed inside her fist, and pulled him to her. Palmer tripped forward in surprise, but met her lips in a kiss. Ariana reached behind him and slammed the door. She backed toward her bed, kissing him all the while, then turned around and shoved him down, so that his back was to the bed, and his face would be clear to the camera.

Palmer looked up at her, surprised, but clearly pleased. Ariana could practically see him through the view screen on her phone—see how perfectly he was framed, how clear his face was in the picture. Swallowing back the nauseated feeling rising up in her throat, Ariana lay down on top of him, but quickly rolled off to the right side so that her back was to the wall. So that she wasn't blocking the camera's view of his face.

Palmer smiled, his eyes never leaving hers. He reached his hand up, cupped her face, and gently kissed her. Ariana's fingers clenched. He was so sweet. So gentle. So freaking unsuspecting.

I can't do this. I can't, I can't, I can't.

But you have to. You must. You must get into Stone and Grave.

Ariana steeled herself. There was a task at hand. All she had to do was complete the task. Then she wouldn't have to worry about it anymore. It would all be over if she could just get through the next few minutes. And a few minutes were really all she had. The digital card on her phone would be full before she knew it.

She pulled back, sat up, and tore off her sweater, revealing the skimpy tank top underneath. Palmer smiled and took his shirt off too, showing off his very ripped chest and stomach. The next ten minutes were a blur. Ariana kept trying to concentrate on Palmer, kept trying to shove her own betrayal into the back of her mind. But she couldn't do it. All she could think about while he kissed her and touched her and undressed her was the fact that a camera was running. The fact that someone in Stone and Grave was going to demand to see the recording. Someone else—possibly Lexa—was going to watch every second of what was happening.

Unless . . .

Did it really have to be every second?

Ariana pulled back from Palmer's kisses.

"What's the matter?" he asked, breathless.

"Nothing. I just . . . I forgot. Lillian's supposed to be back soon," Ariana said, yanking her shirt over her head and rolling away from Palmer.

"Seriously?" he asked, sitting up. His face was flushed and he was practically panting. Ariana was flattered by the fact that he was so attracted to her that he was already that far gone.

"Yeah. I'm sorry. I totally forgot," Ariana said as she smoothed her hair. "Can we go back to your room?"

Palmer blinked a few times. He plucked his sweatshirt off the floor and pulled it on. "Um . . . yeah. Sure. Landon's at some record company meeting tonight."

"Cool. Let's go," Ariana said, taking his hand.

"Okay," Palmer said, still in a stupor.

Ariana led Palmer out of the room, leaving the camera behind, feeling giddy over the fact that it wouldn't be recording the ending of this encounter, wherever it may lead. Feeling, for the first time in days, like she had the power.

NEW TASK

"Tap number three. What is the birthplace of Stone and Grave brother Rabbit?" Conrad demanded, staring down at Ariana. His nostrils flared and her heart pounded a nervous beat. It was amazing how intimidated she felt in front of him, when just a few hours ago they were laughing together in class over an odd turn of phrase in Hamlet.

"Brooklyn, New York, Brother Lear," she replied, her legs quaking beneath her. For the past hour, Ariana and her fellow taps had been kneeling on the floor in the Tombs, their knees pressed into the icy concrete, their burlap sacks chafing their bare skin. Never in her life would Ariana have been able to predict how difficult it was to kneel for that long, but her thigh muscles had started quivering about half an hour earlier, begging for her to sit back on her heels, to stand up, to lay down—anything to relieve them.

"What do you think you're doing, plebe?!" Conrad shouted suddenly, spittle flying from his lips as he turned on Tahira.

Ariana was so startled she almost collapsed. Tahira pushed herself up into her kneeling position with her fingertips to the ground. Clearly she had tried to sit back for a second.

"Sorry. I . . . I just needed a break," she stammered.

Ariana had never seen Tahira be anything less than firm, focused, and in charge. Stammering was not her style.

"What makes you think you deserve a break!?" Conrad shouted, his eyes nearly popping out of his skull. "I see you move again and you're out on your ass."

Ariana felt her heartbeat in every inch of her body. She tightened her glutes and thighs and they whimpered in response. This was torture. Plain and simple. But she wasn't going to move. No way was she going to invite Conrad and his psycho tirade to her end of the line. She breathed in and briefly closed her eyes. At times like these, she couldn't help thinking of Noelle and Kiran and Taylor and wonder what they were doing at that precise moment. Whatever it was, she knew that they would agree with her—this was no way to spend a Friday night.

"Tap number four," Conrad continued, shouting down at Jasper. "What is the Stone and Grave nickname of Maria Stanzini?"

"Estella, Brother Lear," Jasper replied quickly.

"Tap number five," Conrad said, pacing over to Kaitlynn. "Is Oswald your real last name?"

Ariana's throat closed and she turned her head to look at Kaitlynn. Up until that moment, every question posed for the past hour had been straight out of the Stone and Grave handbook—which Lear had updated once the rest of the members had revealed themselves. This was the first personal question anyone had been asked. The implications were clear. Stone and Grave was still trying to find information on Kaitlynn's family, and they were still, of course, coming up blank.

"Eyes forward, tap number three!" April shouted. She was standing off to the side as Conrad quizzed the pledges, but she stepped forward now, her green eyes flashing. Ariana whipped her head to face front, her heart bouncing around erratically in her chest.

"I'm not at liberty to say," Kaitlynn replied.

"Tap number five! Stone and Grave cannot admit a pledge if we can't be certain we even know her true name!" Conrad shouted. "Tell me! What is your true name?"

Ariana's mind felt hazy. A tingling sensation began at the back of her skull and clouded over her vision. She was going to faint. Right here and now. She wondered whether the Stone and Grave could admit a pledge who dropped unconscious at the first threat to a fellow tap.

There was a sudden slam and Ariana's brain instantly cleared. The sound of scurried footsteps preceded Soomie's panicked entrance into the Tombs. She raced over to Conrad and April, her dark hair wild, her eyes wide.

"You guys! The headstones . . . they're gone!" she gasped.

The few Stone and Grave members who were milling around, half-heartedly watching the pledges' interrogation—apparently this was not a required ritual for the membership—moved forward. Palmer emerged from behind the stacks and Ariana's heart filled with longing. She hadn't even realized he was there. Now she wanted to reach out and grip his leg for support. She would have killed just to stand up and fall into his arms.

Just that morning, Ariana had spent her entire free period reviewing the video she'd taken of the two of them on her phone, trying to find the perfect still shot to grab from it. The idea had come to her in the middle of their hook-up. A still-shot of Palmer in a compromising position was just as good as a video, and the task card hadn't stipulated live footage. After an hour of replaying the five-minute video over and over and over again, Ariana had managed to find a tawdry-looking still in which they were both bare-chested, her back to the screen, and Palmer was kissing her neck. She'd saved it, cropped it, printed it out, and sealed it in an envelope. Now all she had to do was deliver it to Stone and Grave, which she planned to do on Halloween—at the very last minute. No reason to incur whatever consequences would come of this until she absolutely had to. But at least she wouldn't need to use the video. She could take comfort in that.

And Palmer could too. Although he didn't know that yet. Still, she had to believe that he would want her to complete her task, at whatever cost. That her being in Stone and Grave with him was an end that would justify the means.

"What do you mean, they're gone?" Palmer asked Soomie.

"I just went to get them out for our ritual tomorrow, and they're not there," Soomie said, throwing a hand up. "Every last one of them is gone. They've been stolen. I found this on the floor of the closet." She handed Palmer an ivory note card. He opened it, read it, and went ashen as he held it out for the other guys to see.

"Freaking Fellows," Rob said under his breath.

Kaitlynn ever so slowly raised her hand.

"What is it, tap number five?" Conrad snapped.

"Sorry, Brother Lear. But . . . what headstones?" Kaitlynn asked.

Ariana rolled her eyes at Kaitlynn's audacity. Conrad had been just about to kick the girl out of the Tombs and now she was asking questions of the membership?

"Our ritual headstones," April explained. "They have our Stone and Grave names on them. We use them at all official rituals."

"Remember? From the woods?" Tahira said under her breath.

"Oh. Right," Kaitlynn said. "So the Fellows took them?"

"You are to address us by our Stone and Grave names," April admonished.

"Sorry, Sister Miss Temple," Kaitlynn said, coloring slightly. "Brother Starbuck, did the Fellows take them?" she asked Palmer.

"Looks that way," Palmer said, tipping the card. "Tsang does love his rhymes."

"Brother Starbuck, is that a clue?" Jasper asked, lifting his chin and inching forward on his knees, as if he could possibly see it from his position on the floor.

"Yeah. And it's a riddle, of course," Palmer replied. He held the card up and read it aloud.

"Small and dark and cramped am I, though never you would know.
For only one may enter to my secret lair below.
All honored memories locked inside,
And now your precious gifts I hide.
Prostrate and apologize
Or perish your names in a fiery glow."

He folded the card and looked around at the other Stone and Grave members as well as the taps. For a long moment, silence reigned inside the Tombs.

"Anyone know what that means?" Palmer asked.

Conrad, Rob, and Soomie all looked at one another blankly.

"Well, the end is pretty clear," April said, reaching for the card. "Tsang wants us to bow down to him and apologize for the gum prank, or he's going to destroy the headstones."

"That asshole," Rob said through his teeth.

"We need those headstones," Palmer said. "They're a huge part of Stone and Grave ritual. If anything happens to them, or worse, if they're publicly revealed, our alumni will kill us. They may even shut down our chapter."

Ariana glanced at Kaitlynn. Shut down the chapter?

"I can work on it," April offered, tucking the riddle into her jeans pocket under her robe. "I'm pretty good at word play."

"Good. Do that," Palmer said. "You figure out that riddle, Miss Temple, and you'll save Stone and Grave."

Ariana's heart fluttered and suddenly she knew what she had to do. She had to solve that riddle herself. If she did, *she* would be the one to save the APH chapter of Stone and Grave. And if she could do that, she was sure her task would no longer matter. Wouldn't rescuing the entire chapter from ruin trump handing in a stupid photo of one of their own members fooling around with his secret girlfriend? It would have to.

Talk about killing two birds with one stone. Or, more accurately, *saving* two birds—her chapter and her relationship. Ariana smiled slowly, even as her leg muscles cramped in anguish, radiating fingers of pain up her back.

This time tomorrow, she was going to be a Stone and Grave superstar.

THE RIDDLE

"Thanks for gracing us with your presence," Ariana said tersely as Tahira trudged into study room A at the library on Saturday morning.

Tahira tugged off her dark sunglasses and shot Ariana an irritated look as she slid into one of the wooden chairs around the conference-style table, right next to Kaitlynn. Her face was, for once, completely free of makeup, and her dark hair was wavy and wild beneath a gray cloche hat.

"Sorry, but seven a.m. on a Saturday is kind of early for me," she said, plucking her hat off her head and tossing it in front of Landon's crossed arms.

Landon's eyes were at half-mast, his cheeks stubbly. Only Jasper and Kaitlynn looked as if they'd bothered to shower before showing up for Ariana's secret meeting. Jasper's blond hair was still wet and slicked back from his face and Kaitlynn had actually bothered to apply a little eyeliner and lip gloss.

"What are we doing here, anyway?" Tahira asked. "Your e-mail was seriously cryptic."

Ariana folded her hands on the table, feeling very in charge and very proud of herself. She looked around at each of her fellow taps and smiled. "I have an idea that may keep the rest of us from getting cut from Stone and Grave."

Kaitlynn's eyebrows shot up and Tahira shifted forward in her seat. Even Landon suddenly blinked his eyes all the way open, truly awake for the first time.

"Really?" Jasper asked, lowering his forearm flat on the table. "What, pray tell, might this be?"

"All we have to do is solve Martin Tsang's riddle and retrieve the headstones on our own," Ariana said quietly, urgently. "If we do that, the membership will be so grateful they'll let every last one of us in."

Landon sat up straight, tossing his bangs back from his face. He and the other taps all looked around at each other, pondering the idea. "I like it," he said, his voice scratchy. "But do you really think we can do it?"

"Yeah," Tahira said. "We don't even have the poem."

"True, but I thought that between the five of us, we might remember all the important parts," Ariana replied.

"I memorized it," Kaitlynn said, raising her hand to shoulder level.

"You did?" Ariana asked.

"I have a photographic memory," Kaitlynn said, lifting her chin smugly.

Ariana stared at her. She was learning new things about Kaitlynn every day. She slipped a notebook and pen out of her bag, opened the book to a clean page, and poised the pen over it. The others followed suit. All but Landon, who hadn't thought to bring anything with him. He gave Ariana a sheepish look and dropped back in his chair, his hair falling back over his eyes.

"Well? Were you planning to share?" Jasper said.

Kaitlynn took a breath and recited, pausing between each line to give the others time to jot them down. She was biting back a smile throughout the recitation, clearly relishing her pertinent role in the proceedings.

"'Small and dark and cramped am I, though never you would know. . . .'"

Kaitlynn ran through the entire riddle, while the others sat transfixed.

"Thanks, Lily," Ariana said when Kaitlynn was finished.

"Anytime," Kaitlynn replied with a proud smile.

Ariana quickly scrawled the last few words, then sat back to read it over. "Okay. So we're looking for a small, dark, and cramped room," she began.

"Probably a basement," Jasper added, chewing on the inside of his cheek. "Since it says it has a secret lair below."

"The Tombs?" Landon said with a yawn, lacing his fingers together on the table.

"Why would they hide our headstones in our own secret meeting place?" Tahira snapped.

"I dunno," Landon said, parting his palms. "I'm just saying. It's a secret lair, and it's down below."

"And it *is* dark, but it's not cramped or small," Ariana put in. "Those stacks go on for miles."

"So does anyone know of any other basement rooms at APH?" Kaitlynn asked, looking around. "Storage spaces or anything like that?"

"It's probably not a regular storage room though," Ariana corrected. She tapped the cap end of her pen against her chin. "It says there are honored memories locked inside."

"'Honored memories . . . ,'" Tahira mused, pushing her thick hair back from her face with both hands. "Like diaries? Maybe the headmaster's diary or journal or something?"

"I don't know. 'Honored memories . . . ,'" Ariana said, her eyes narrow as she brainstormed. "It makes it sound more important than diaries. More . . . historical, maybe? Like maybe the founders' diaries or something like that?"

"I've got it!" Jasper said, shoving his chair backward with his legs as he stood. The chair made an awful screeching sound against the wood floor, and Ariana's shoulders curled toward her ears. "What about the archives?" he suggested.

Tahira and Landon exchanged a look.

"The archives don't exist," Tahira said with a scoff. "They're a prep school myth."

"But if they did exist, this poem would definitely lead us there, right?" Jasper said, pacing around the table, wielding his copy of the poem. "'Honored memories'? 'Only one may enter'?"

Tahira frowned thoughtfully. "I guess. . . ."

"What are the archives?" Ariana asked, intrigued. "I don't remember them from the campus history or the map."

"That's just it," Jasper said, dropping his notebook on the table and leaning both hands into the back of an empty chair. "The archives don't officially exist."

"Okay. I'm confused. If they don't exist, how can our headstones be there?" Kaitlynn asked, shifting in her chair.

Tahira rolled her eyes and sat forward. "It's this story passed down from one class to the next," she explained. "Supposedly, there's some secret spot on campus where the founders hid all these historical items from around the time the school was founded. Diaries, blueprints, the original school documents . . . plus newspapers and original uniforms. Crap like that."

"Like one huge time capsule," Jasper said, his eyes bright with excitement. "And supposedly each year a senior is gifted with the key to the archives, to keep just in case the faculty member in charge passes on or something."

"Only one may enter," Kaitlynn said, sitting up straight.

"Well, where is it?" Ariana asked, her pulse beginning to skip. "And how do we get the key? I mean, how do we find out who the senior student is?"

Silence reigned inside the study room. Ariana felt her spirits fall. She'd never seen such a perfectly blank slate of expressions.

"Martin Tsang. He's the one student who has a key."

Ariana looked up at the door. Adam Lazerri stood there, hugging himself in his skimpy cotton coat, his dark curls sticking out in all directions.

"Adam? What are you doing here?" Ariana asked, her throat dry. Adam shouldn't be privy to inside information. She and her fellow taps could get in huge trouble for this. Immense trouble.

"I followed you guys," he said, his Adam's apple bobbing up and down as he took a tentative step into the room. "When I saw Landon and Jasper walk out together, I knew it had to have something to do with Stone and Grave," he said. "I've been standing outside the room listening this entire time," he added, tilting his head toward the door.

Ariana's spirits sagged. Rule number one in clandestine meetings: Always close the door.

"You shouldn't be here, dude," Landon said, sitting up straight. "You're going to get us all kicked out."

"Wait," Jasper said. "Has it escaped everyone's attention that Adam just said he knows something about the riddle?"

Ariana glanced at Kaitlynn, who stared back, determined. Clearly she was ready to use Adam for whatever information he had. And for once, Ariana couldn't have agreed with her more.

"Get in here and close the door," she told Adam.

Adam did as he was told, but didn't remove his jacket or sit down. He stood in the corner of the small room, looking awkward with his hands down at his sides. His skin was pale and there were dark circles under his eyes, as if he hadn't slept in days. Ariana's heart went out to him. She knew he was still hurting over Brigit. Plus, Adam was here on scholarship. Getting into Stone and Grave probably meant more to him than it did the others. The society meant connections he otherwise had no hope of making, considering his meager background.

"I don't like this," Tahira said. "He can't know what's going on with Stone and Grave. There's a reason it's called a secret society."

"Did you guys really think it was fair, the way I got thrown out?" Adam asked, his voice quiet but firm. "I mean, just because I don't run as fast as Landon, I'm cut? Seriously?"

No one replied. Ariana was sure they were all trying to weigh the risks of Adam being here against the potential rewards.

"I just want a chance to prove to them that I'm worth taking a second look, that's all," Adam said, stepping forward. "And I know I can help you guys."

Ariana took a deep breath. "Okay. You say Martin Tsang is the one with the key to the archives. How do you know that?"

"Tsang is like the right-hand man of Dr. Tomassen," Adam said. "The head of the history department. The two of us are always there together, working on special projects for the teachers, filing, cleaning out old tests and stuff, but he never misses a chance to remind me that he's more important than I am. One day we were talking and he started showing off about how much Tomassen trusts him. How he entrusted him with the biggest secret in the entire school."

"He told you about the archives?" Tahira said dubiously.

"Not exactly, but I know that's what he was talking about. What else could it be?" Adam said, lifting his shoulders. "And then, one night, when we were working late, Tomassen came and pulled Martin out. I was sick of his ego trip crap, so I followed them, and I saw Tomassen give him something. I heard him say that one current student is granted this honor each year—that he had to protect whatever it was, just in case anything happens to Tomassen. It must've been a key to the archives."

Ariana was breathless. This was it. It had to be.

"What's Martin keeping there?" Adam asked. He blushed sheepishly. "I missed that part."

Tahira clenched her jaw and looked away. Ariana was just debating whether to tell him, when Jasper beat her to it.

"They took our headstones," he said. "We're going to get them back."

"Jasper!" Landon admonished, his cheeks flushed with anger.

"We still don't know *where* the archives are," Kaitlynn pointed out, ignoring Landon.

"Follow Tsang," Adam said, his posture straightening. "I'd bet money that he hangs out at the archives every chance he gets. I'm sure it makes him feel all special, the fact that he's the only one with a key. And he'd definitely be there if he was keeping something of Stone and Grave's there."

"So follow Tsang . . . find the stones," Jasper said, looking at Ariana.

Ariana grinned at him. "It's time for a stakeout."

FELLOW SCHEMER

Ariana tugged her black wool hat down over her ears as she knelt in the dirt next to Jasper. The two of them were huddled behind a large rock, about fifty yards away from the back door of Pryce Hall. Behind the tree to her right were Tahira and Landon, and crouched behind another rock were Kaitlynn and Adam, all of them dressed in head-to-toe black. The debate over whether to include Adam had raged for an hour before Jasper had suggested a vote and Tahira and Landon had been outnumbered. Ariana knew it was a risk, but she agreed with Adam. He hadn't deserved to be thrown out so offhandedly. And it was too late anyway. He already knew what was going on. Besides, without him, they wouldn't have even gotten as far as they had.

"Are we sure this is where the archives are?" Ariana whispered.

"Adam and I took shifts watching Martin Tsang all day," Jasper replied, tugging a pair of high-tech binoculars from his waistband. Ariana had no idea where he'd gotten them, and she decided she didn't care. She was just glad he had them. "He went in through this door three different times, and Adam saw a couple of Fellows come out right before lunch. Then *after* lunch I saw two others go in. That's why we think there might be more than one of them guarding the stones. It's like they're taking shifts."

He lifted the binoculars to his eyes and adjusted the knobs. "Yes. We have movement," he said, handing over the binocs. "Check the westernmost window."

Ariana stared him down. "You can just say right or left."

He smirked, his blond bangs sticking out from beneath the hem of his black hat. "Left."

Ariana rolled her eyes and checked the window. Linen blinds were pulled securely over the windows to discourage prying eyes, but the lights were on inside, and sure enough, Ariana could see the shadows of two or more people moving around behind them.

"Okay. Are you ready to do this?" Ariana asked.

Jasper lifted his stuffed backpack onto his shoulders. "Say the word, General Covington."

Ariana stifled a laugh and stood up. "Everyone," she whisper-shouted. "We're going in!"

Tentatively, Landon, Tahira, Adam, and Kaitlynn slipped out of their hiding places, each toting a large bag, some empty for carrying back the headstones, others full of the creative weaponry needed for Jasper's plan. The six of them crouched and ran, two by two, across the open grass between the tree line and the back of Pryce Hall.

"Get down!" Jasper whispered as they reached the outer wall.

Ariana hit the ground, her back up against the cold brick wall, the branches of the decorative shrubbery around the building scratching at her knees. Tahira and Landon ended up on one side of the metal door, Ariana, Jasper, Kaitlynn, and Adam on the other. For a few moments, no one moved a muscle. Ariana's heart pounded in her throat and in her temples. If the Fellows realized they were here before they wanted the Fellows to know, their plan was done for. And the headstones might be done for too. All of this was being done to impress the Stone and Grave membership, but they would not be impressed if the taps frightened the Fellows into destroying the stones prematurely.

"Okay. Is everyone clear on their assignments?" Ariana whispered.

The others nodded. Jasper and Landon pulled several bottles of canola oil from their bags, stolen from the dining hall earlier that day. Tahira jimmied out a couple of torn feather pillows. A few white feathers escaped into the breeze. Ariana and Kaitlynn followed suit, carefully extracting their own pillows. Ariana clutched the tear closed to keep from making too much of a mess.

"Let's go!" Jasper whispered.

He got up and, ever so quietly, tugged open the heavy back door. He held it as Ariana, Tahira, Landon, Kaitlynn, then Adam slipped through, then closed it slowly—silently.

Ariana tiptoed down the stairs, her leg muscles tense, the others following her lead. At the bottom of the steps, she found a perfectly round, empty room with a gleaming marble floor. To the right was a heavy wooden door with an imposing-looking bronze doorknob and an ancient keyhole. She held up a hand as the others fell in behind her on the stairs. A loud round of laughter sounded on the other side of the door.

"They're in there," she whispered.

"Quiet, everyone," Jasper added. "This is it. Take your positions."

Ariana, Tahira, and Kaitlynn tiptoed around the room, spacing themselves out evenly along the walls, still clutching their pillows. Landon, Adam, and Jasper opened up their bottles of oil and, starting at the top of the room and working their way backward toward the door to the archives, dumped their contents out all over the floor. Ariana scrunched her nose as the scent of oil filled the room, the glug-glug of the bottles sounding like a trumpet call in the silence. Every second she expected the Fellows to come through the door and into the foyer to check out the noise, but the door stayed shut. Finally, the bottles were empty. Jasper shoved the plastic bottles into his bag and placed it against the wall by the door to the archives. Then he pressed his back up against the wall. Landon and Adam stood on the opposite side of the door.

"Everyone ready?" Jasper whispered.

Ariana held her breath and nodded with the others. Jasper met her eye. "Go!"

Jasper, Landon, and Adam pounded on the door and shouted, making a huge cacophony in the silence. It took about half a second for the door to fling open, nearly knocking Jasper off his feet. Four of the Fellows came barreling out and instantly slipped on the oily floor. The first went flying heels-over-head and landed directly on his back. The second tripped over his friend's prone body and fell face-first into the thick of the oil, sliding clear across the floor. The third and fourth saw what had happened to their brethren and tried to stop short, but they were too late. They skidded forward, collided with one another, and were sent sprawling in a fit of shouts and groans.

"Feathers!" Jasper shouted to the girls. "Now! Go! Go! Go!" he prodded Landon and Adam.

The guys ran into the now-open archive room while Ariana, Kaitlynn, and Tahira stepped tentatively forward, staying on the oil-free periphery, and shook out their feather pillows. White fluff filled the room and fluttered down all over the four Fellows, sticking fast to their oil-slicked bodies. Ariana felt a laugh bubble up in her throat as the Fellows struggled to get up onto their hands and knees, only to splay out flat again, cursing and vowing to kill the girls. Soon she, Tahira, and Kaitlynn were all laughing together, adding more and more feathers to the mess and confusing the Fellows to the ends of their wits. She met Tahira's and Kaitlynn's eyes through the thick air and realized she was actually enjoying this, enjoying doing this with them. Little did the Fellows know that their ill-conceived prank was actually working to bring the Stone and Grave taps closer.

"We've got them!" Jasper shouted as he, Adam, and Landon emerged from the archives. Their backpacks were stuffed to the gills, unzipped at the top with a few stones jutting out of each. Apparently the stones weren't stones at all, but made of some lightweight material, because the guys seemed to be having no trouble toting them.

"Let's go!" Ariana replied. "Stick to the walls."

The guys followed her instructions, sidestepping toward her with their backs to the bricks. The girls joined them. As they made it to the stairs, one of the Fellows managed to scramble to his feet. His legs slid out on both sides, but he threw his arms out and kept his balance. He was completely covered in white and brown feathers—his hair, his hands, his lips—and his chest heaved as he pressed his fingers into fists. This guy was pissed off.

"You are *so* dead," he said through his teeth.

"Spread the word," Ariana said, laughing. "The Stone and Grave is not to be trifled with."

Then she balled up her pillowcase and threw it at him. He reached for it instinctively and, in doing so, lost his balance and slammed to the floor with a splat. Ariana and her friends cracked up laughing and ran up the stairs, tripping out into the night.

"Nice one," Jasper said as they jogged away from the door.

"Please. That was all you," Ariana said breathlessly. She paused as they reached the tree line and bent to catch her breath. The others raced ahead, intent on getting as far away from the building as possible.

"I guess we both have wicked minds," Jasper replied, leaning one hand against a thick tree trunk as he sucked wind.

"What do you mean?" Ariana asked. She tugged her hat off and shook her hair out, her scalp tingling.

"The gum thing? I know that was your idea," Jasper said, taking a step toward her. "It was noble, what you tried to do for Lillian . . . but I know a fellow schemer when I see one."

Ariana's face fell at being snagged, but then she slowly smiled. It was nice to have her idea acknowledged. For a long moment, she and Jasper stood there together, under the canopy of branches, catching their breath and smiling.

"Come on. Let's go reap our spoils," he said finally.

And together, they took off after their friends.

CREDIT WHERE CREDIT IS DUE

Ariana and her fellow taps all lined up in tap order in the Tombs—
Tahira at position one, Kaitlynn at five, Ariana right in the center at
number three—standing in the spots in which they were normally
placed for Stone and Grave interrogations. On the floor behind them
were the bags full of headstones. Each of the taps stood with their
hands clenched behind their backs, and Ariana felt as if she could hear
the hearts of her cohorts pounding with excitement. When she heard
the door squeal open in the distance, followed by a bevy of confused,
intense voices, she found she could hardly breathe.

This was going to work. It had to.

The first person to enter the room was Lexa. Her jaw dropped
slightly when she saw the taps standing there, but she quickly recov-
ered and stormed over. She was wearing jeans and a sweater under
her red coat. Her face was scrubbed clean, and there was a crease on
her right cheek from her pillow. Ariana felt a twinge of satisfaction,

knowing her text to the membership had woken Lexa up.

"You? You called this meeting?" she demanded, looking down the line of pledges. "And what the hell is Adam doing here?"

"If you don't mind, Sister Becky Sharp, we'd like to wait for the entire membership to arrive before we explain," Ariana replied coolly. She was not going to let Lexa intimidate her. Right now, Ariana had the power.

Lexa's green eyes flashed. "Do *not* use that name in front of him," she snapped, thrusting a finger out at Adam. "How dare you bring an outsider in here? This is sacred space."

Ariana could feel Landon and Tahira staring her down. Her face burned under their accusatory glares, but she didn't flinch. She was in the right here. And she wasn't about to let them think otherwise. Soon the Tombs were filled with Stone and Grave brothers and sisters, all of whom were staring the taps up and down, murmuring and whispering. Lexa narrowed her eyes at Ariana.

"Well, it appears we're all here now . . . at *your* request," Lexa said with a sneer. "Why don't you give me one good reason not to throw all six of you out on your asses right now?"

"We've got about thirty," Jasper replied.

He, Ariana, and Landon turned, picked up the backpacks full of Stone and Grave headstones, and placed them at Lexa's feet. April stepped forward out of the crowd, her red hair back in a ponytail, her coat tied loosely over flannel pajamas, and she gaped down at the bags, dumbstruck.

"Are those—?"

Lexa bent and tugged one of the stones from the first bag. Then she and April unzipped all of them and dumped them out carefully onto the floor, laying them out in front of the taps.

"How did you . . . where did you . . . ?" April stuttered. "I haven't even cracked the riddle yet."

Palmer slipped out from the huddle of members wearing gray sweatpants and a navy blue Yale sweatshirt. He knelt down to inspect the stones. "Someone start explaining," he said, looking up at Landon. "Now."

"Brother Starbu—," Kaitlynn began. Then, off a silencing glare from Lexa, her mouth snapped shut. She cleared her throat and started again. "If I may speak?"

Lexa nodded. "Go ahead."

"Ana thought it would be good for us to take initiative and retrieve the stones," Kaitlynn said. "As a gesture to you . . . our brothers and sisters. She called the tap class together and she and Jasper figured out the riddle."

"Is this true?" Lexa said to Ariana.

Ariana was so dumbfounded over the fact that Kaitlynn had just given her credit where credit was due—that she hadn't even mentioned her own role in the riddle-solving—she could hardly find her voice. Her body tingled with warmth from the top of her head all the way to the tips of her toes. It was in that moment that she knew all of her plotting had worked. She and Kaitlynn were friends again. Really and truly friends.

"Yes," she said, unable to contain her grin. "It's true." Then she took a breath and continued. "But Lillian was the one who remembered the riddle word for word," she added. "And if it wasn't for Adam, we would have gotten nowhere with the answer. We never would have found the archives without him."

"The archives?" Palmer said, standing up and turning to Adam. "They exist?"

"They do," Jasper replied as Adam blushed in silence. "And thanks to Adam, we now know exactly where they are."

"The Fellows were keeping our headstones there," Ariana explained.

"'All honored memories locked inside, and now your precious gifts I hide,'" April recited, crossing her arms over her chest. "Of course."

"The archives made sense, but it was Adam who came forward with the information that Martin Tsang had a key to get inside," Ariana explained. "We followed Tsang and we found the stones."

"Okay, but how did you get him to give them back?" Palmer asked, crossing his arms over his chest and eyeing them with interest.

Ariana looked at Jasper and laughed. "It's a long story," Jasper said. "But let's just say they didn't give them up willingly."

"Let's just say it was a . . . sticky situation," Kaitlynn added.

Palmer smirked and Ariana could tell he wanted the whole story, but she and the other taps were still on the hot seat, and now didn't seem like the moment for a hilarious retelling of the details.

"I still don't understand how Adam got involved," Lexa said suspiciously. "I thought we made it clear that this is a *secret* society. How many outsiders, exactly, did you go to for help?"

"They didn't come to me. I followed them," Adam spoke up

finally. "I wanted to prove to them, and to all of you, that I deserve to be here. It's not their fault I listened in." He paused and smiled, lifting an eyebrow. "I'm just that good."

Palmer and a few of the other guys laughed, but they stopped short at a stern look from Lexa. She turned around and walked over to the first dusty bookcase, gripping the shelf in front of her with both hands, clearly deep in thought. Ariana held her breath. Would Lexa really kick all of them out? Could the Atherton-Pryce Hall chapter of Stone and Grave really justify having no pledge class at all?

Finally, Lexa lifted her head and turned to face the membership, her back to the taps. A bolt of apprehension sizzled through Ariana's heart.

"Brothers and sisters, tonight our tap class has proven that we have been wise in our selections this semester," she said loudly. Then she glanced over her shoulder at Adam. "And, perhaps, too hasty in some of our decisions."

Adam grinned from ear to ear.

"To our taps!" Lexa shouted, raising one arm in the air.

"To our taps!" the membership shouted back.

Ariana's heart inflated with happiness as the entire room dissolved into applause and cheers and congratulations. A couple of the guys clapped Adam on the back and pulled him into the group. Maria and Soomie, meanwhile, raced forward to hug her, which made it all the easier to hug Palmer as well without looking suspicious. As he grabbed her up in his arms and lifted her off her feet, Ariana had never felt so free, so accomplished, and so proud.

She'd done it. She'd gotten the headstones back to Stone and Grave and, thanks to Kaitlynn, she'd gotten most of the credit for it. There was no way they were going to hold her to her task now. She and Palmer were going to remain a secret until they were ready to come out as a couple, and she was going to go down in history as the Stone and Grave tap who'd saved their headstones.

Everything was working out even better than planned.

DRESSING UP

Ariana couldn't stop smiling. And since she couldn't remember the last time she couldn't stop smiling, she decided to relish it. As she, Palmer, Kaitlynn, and Jasper walked into Privilege House together, shaking off the chill of the night air, she caught a glimpse of her grinning reflection in the window and it only made her smile wider.

"You guys have no idea what this has done for your stock," Palmer said as they walked into the elevator alcove. Jasper hit the up buttons for both the girls' and boys' elevators. "We're talking through the roof."

"Deservedly so, I think," Jasper said as Kaitlynn and Ariana laughed happily.

"I just can't believe we solved the riddle before April did," Ariana said.

"I can," Palmer said, eyeing her with pride. "And nice job with the execution, man," he said, turning to Jasper. "I just wish you guys had thought to take some video. I'd give anything to see those guys flailing around covered in feathers."

"Video!" Kaitlynn said. "Why didn't we think of that?"

Possibly because I never want to think about video-recording anything ever again, Ariana thought.

"Next time," Jasper promised.

"There's going to be a next time?" Palmer said with a laugh.

"Never say never," Jasper replied mischievously.

The elevators pinged at the same time and Kaitlynn and Jasper moved to get in. Ariana started to follow her roommate, but Palmer grazed her arm with his fingers.

"Ana. Hang back for a sec," he said.

Ariana glanced at Kaitlynn in her elevator, and Kaitlynn smirked knowingly. Then she looked at Jasper just as the doors closed on him. His sour look wasn't lost on her, but she chose not to think about what it might mean.

"What's up?" she asked Palmer once the others were being whisked off to their floors. "The next group will be along any minute."

The members of Stone and Grave had decided to leave the library in shifts since it was well past midnight, and four people at a time would be able to move a bit more stealthily than a group of thirty-plus.

"I know. C'mere," Palmer said, smiling adorably and tilting his head toward the lobby's common room.

Her heart skipping, Ariana followed him inside and let him tug her into a private corner. He slipped his arms around her waist, leaned down, and kissed her. It was a nice, long, deep, familiar kiss. The kind of perfect kiss a boyfriend gives to his girlfriend. When he pulled away, Ariana leaned into his chest and grinned up at him.

"So, I was just wondering . . . do you have a costume for the Halloween party yet?" Palmer asked, resting the back of his head against the wall behind him.

"No. Not really," Ariana said with a sigh. "Lily and I were thinking about doing something together, but we haven't come up with anything good yet."

"Cool. Because if you think Lily wouldn't mind, I was thinking *we* should do something together," Palmer said, adjusting his arms on her hips and pulling her even closer.

Ariana, however, found herself stepping away from him. "You mean like a couples' costume?"

Palmer's brow creased. They heard the lock on the front door of Privilege House click and boisterous laughter followed. Ariana turned and moved further into the room toward the movie theater. She leaned back against the wall, out of sight of the lobby, trying to figure out how to turn Palmer down gently.

"Yeah, I mean a couples costume," Palmer whispered, following her. He stood facing her, but a couple of feet away now—keeping his distance. "Why not?"

"I don't know. Isn't that kind of . . . public?" Ariana asked, shoving her hands into the pockets of her coat.

Palmer blew out a sigh toward his forehead, fanning out his bangs. "Is this about Lexa again? Because from what I can tell, she and Conrad are getting serious. *They're* even dressing up together— as a married couple! The girl has definitely moved on."

"I know, but . . . Palmer, I need to be careful. Especially now," Ariana said.

"What do you mean, especially now? Because she's president of Stone and Grave?" Palmer whispered, glancing toward the open door. In the alcove, the elevators pinged and the voices quickly disappeared. "Ana, she's always *been* the president of Stone and Grave. The only difference is . . . now you know it."

"Right. And now that I know it, I can't stop thinking about it," Ariana said. "If she still has any kind of feelings for you, I can't make her mad. Not right now."

Palmer laughed, tipping his head back. "Dude. After tonight you don't even need to worry about that. There's no way any of you are getting cut. Especially not you. The whole thing was your idea. You're a lock."

Looking down at the carpeted floor, Ariana felt the smile twitching at her lips again. But she couldn't get complacent and rest on her laurels. She'd made that mistake in the past and it always got her in trouble. When she'd been less than vigilant back at Easton, Reed had ended up finding that stupid photo of Thomas on Kiran's phone and before Ariana knew it she'd lost everything. Her friends, her school, her freedom—her whole identity.

Palmer stepped forward and tugged Ariana's hand from her pocket, holding it lightly in his. "Listen, I'm going to go to the party as Frankenstein. I think it'd be cool if you dressed up as Frankenstein's bride. We don't even have to go together. Just come as the bride. Then I'll know for sure that you're into this," he said, squeezing her palm.

Ariana swallowed hard. "And if I dress up as something else?"

He dropped her hand, stepped back, and shoved his hands into his own pockets. A chill dashed down Ariana's spine.

"Look, Ana. This sneaking around thing isn't working for me

anymore," he said. "All I want is to be with you." He ducked his head, forcing her to look up into his eyes. "So just . . . be my bride . . . okay?"

Ariana stared back at him, unable to take the leap he wanted her to take. At least not yet. She needed Stone and Grave. And to get into Stone and Grave, she was sure she needed Lexa's vote.

"I'll see you there," he said.

Then he turned on his heel and walked through the alcove, shoving open the door to the stairwell. Ariana heard it squeal on its hinges, then slam behind him. Her heart heavy, she walked out to the elevators and managed to get one on her own, before the next group returned. When she got back to her room, Kaitlynn was waiting for her on the edge of her bed, still wearing her black spy gear.

"What was that all about?" she asked, her eyes bright.

Ariana sighed hugely and shrugged off her coat. "He wants to dress up as a couple for the party."

"What did you tell him?" Kaitlynn asked.

"I told him I was dressing up with you," Ariana said, putting her coat on its hanger, then sitting down on her own bed to kick off her shoes.

"No way. You have to dress up with him," Kaitlynn said, scooting around on the bed to face Ariana. "We haven't come up with anything yet anyway."

"I know, but we had a deal," Ariana said, lying back to look up at the ceiling.

"So what? There's always next year," Kaitlynn said, a statement that almost brought a smile to Ariana's lips. "I don't mind. Really. I actually saw this Catwoman costume the other day that was totally hot. I can just get that."

"Okay. But it's not just you I'm worried about," Ariana said, rolling over onto her side and propping her cheek up on her palm. "It's—"

"Lexa," Kaitlynn said. "Screw her. She has Conrad."

"I know, but—"

"Ariana Osgood, this is no time to lose your spine," Kaitlynn said, standing up.

"Shhhhh!" Ariana said, glancing at the door. Kaitlynn had shouted her real name a bit too loudly for comfort.

"I'm just saying," Kaitlynn hissed. "Palmer does not belong to Lexa. Besides. It's about time someone around here put that uppity bitch in her place."

Ariana's gut twisted. Her instinct was to defend Lexa. She'd never agreed with Kaitlynn's negative assessment of her friend. But lately . . . all that had changed a bit. Lexa *had* started acting kind of uppity over the past week. Like she was better than Ariana.

"Maybe you're right," she said noncommittally.

"I know I am," Kaitlynn replied, walking into her closet to change. "And by the time Halloween rolls around, I'll convince you I am."

Ariana laughed. "We'll see."

"You will," Kaitlynn said, peeking her head out from the doorway of her closet. "I'll convince you if it's the last thing I do."

THE LAST WORD

There wasn't much Ariana hated more than jogging, but when Lexa had stopped by her room early that morning wearing her running gear, she couldn't turn down the invitation. It was the perfect opportunity to feel her out. To see if last night's success had done the job and gotten her excused from her task. So now her lungs were burning, her legs were quivering, and her nose was starting to drip from the cold. But it was all going to be worth it. If she could only find the breath needed to converse.

"We should probably get together later and finish our Spanish project," Lexa said, taking the path that led downhill toward the water.

Ariana tried not to groan. Going downhill required strength her legs simply did not possess. Not to mention the fact that going down meant that at some point they were going to have to run back up.

"Definitely," Ariana said breathlessly. "It *is* due tomorrow."

Lexa glanced at her from the corner of her eye, her arms pumping. "I'm aware. That's why I brought it up."

She added a laugh to cover up the obnoxiousness of her statement, and jogged ahead. Lexa was, of course, not in the least bit winded. She did this run almost every morning, rain or shine. Ariana narrowed her eyes at the girl's back and pushed herself to catch up as they reached the concrete jogging trail along the riverbank.

Okay. Just ask her, Ariana told herself, glancing at Lexa out of the corner of her eye. *"So Lexa,"* she practiced silently. *"I don't really have to complete my task now, do I? Saving the whole chapter has to count for more than one little chore. . . ."*

She was just opening her mouth to speak when Lexa interrupted her.

"So. How's your task coming?" Lexa asked, slowing her steps slightly to keep pace with Ariana.

Ariana's stomach dropped and she stopped running completely. She bent forward at the waist, bracing her hands above her knees and fighting for breath.

Sonofabitch, she thought, squeezing her eyes shut. Her lungs felt as if they were on fire and about to launch themselves up her throat and out through her mouth.

Lexa couldn't be serious. She just couldn't be. Ariana had saved the collective ass of the chapter last night. How could they possibly hold her to that stupid task after that?

Lexa ran a few steps ahead before noticing Ariana had dropped off. When she did, she turned around and jogged back, then ran in place next to Ariana, waiting. Ariana stared down at Lexa's Asics sneakers, imagining what might happen if she reached out, grabbed Lexa's ankle, and pulled. Would Lexa fall on her butt? Go sprawling? Crack her head open on the concrete walkway?

"You okay? Did you cramp up?" Lexa asked.

"M'fine," Ariana mumbled at the ground. She sucked in a breath and stood up straight, her hands on her hips. Her side twinged, but she refused to double over again.

"Okay then. Let's go," Lexa said, starting to turn.

"No. I think I'm done here," Ariana replied.

Lexa's expression was annoyed. "Is this about your task?" she asked as she continued to jog in place. "Is there some reason you don't want to complete it? Because as you already know, the rest of your tap class has been done for days."

Suddenly, Ariana's mind felt completely clear, as if the crisp morning air had suddenly filled her skull. Forget April and Conrad. Lexa *had* set the task. Why else would she ask that question? Why couldn't Lexa just release her vise grip on Palmer already? It had been almost two months since the two of them had broken up. Didn't Lexa realize what an awful quality it was—lusting after someone she couldn't have? But that wasn't even the worst of it. The worst of it was that Lexa was lording this over her. Manipulating her. Toying with her emotions. Ariana had thought they were going to be best friends, but instead Lexa was letting something as petty as an ex-boyfriend come between them, and using her position of power over Ariana to do it.

In that moment, she wished Lexa Greene had never existed. If it weren't for her, Ariana's life at Atherton-Pryce would already be exactly the way she wanted it. She'd be the girlfriend of the most popular guy in school with no one to stand in the way of her getting into Stone and Grave.

"I have to go," Ariana said, ignoring Lexa's comment. She turned around and started to storm up the hill.

"Fine. But meet me in my room at two! We have to finish our project!" Lexa shouted after her.

Ariana pressed her lips together and didn't respond. Let the girl have the last word. She clearly thought she deserved to have it.

"Hey, girls! You're just in time," Maria greeted Lexa and Ariana as they arrived at the edge of her plaid picnic blanket after Spanish class on Monday. "Quinn just delivered our coffee and snacks."

"Pumpkin spice latte for Ana, and a skim latte for Lexa," Quinn said, handing over their drinks.

"Thanks," Ariana said, taking her cup and sitting down on the blanket, tucking her pleated skirt modestly around her thighs.

"Thank you, Quinn," Lexa added, sitting as well.

"You're welcome," Quinn said. "I guess I'll be going. Unless you needed something else?"

"We're fine," Maria said dismissively.

Quinn smiled, unaffected by Maria's tone. The girl always simply did her job, no questions asked, no complaints. It was quite admirable, really.

"Okay. See you later." Quinn tugged out her phone as she scurried off, sending a quick text. Of everyone Ariana had met at Atherton-Pryce, Quinn always seemed to be the busiest.

"So? How did your presentation go?" Soomie asked, leaning back against the thick tree trunk behind her.

"Fine," Ariana said.

"Well," Lexa replied at the same time.

They both sipped their coffees and Ariana saw Maria and Soomie exchange a glance. Her skin warmed slightly and she preoccupied herself with straightening her skirt and tugging it down toward her stockinged knees another millimeter. Maria and Soomie weren't stupid. They had to have noticed that things had cooled between her and Lexa.

"So, Ana, have you found out anything else about Lillian and her family?" Lexa asked out of nowhere.

Ariana glanced up at Lexa, her face perfectly framed by her dark hair. Lexa's green eyes studied her shrewdly over the plastic top on her coffee cup.

"I didn't realize I was supposed to be digging," Ariana said.

"Honestly?" Lexa said, raising her perfect eyebrows. "My bad then, I guess. I just assumed after our conversation you would try to get to know her better. I didn't realize I had to spell it out for you."

As if Ariana was so incredibly dense for missing the hint.

"Sorry," Ariana mumbled. She took a sip of her coffee to keep from screaming at Lexa. "I guess I've had a lot on my mind. Maybe you should have made *that* my task. Then there would've been no confusion."

Lexa's eyes flashed and Ariana instantly felt chagrined. What was she thinking, telling Lexa off? Bringing up the task issue in a public forum? She was supposed to be kissing the girl's butt until she got into Stone and Grave. There was no point in keeping her relationship with Palmer a secret if she was just going to irritate Lexa in other ways.

But she already knows about me and Palmer, Ariana thought, frustrated. *Otherwise why would she have set that task?*

She felt like she was playing a game of chicken with Lexa. Neither one wanted to mention the Palmer-Ana relationship out loud first. Well, Ariana was not going to break first. She was not about to ask Lexa's permission to date the guy she loved. Never would she give the girl that satisfaction. When the time was right, everyone would know about Ariana and Palmer, and then Lexa was just going to have to deal with it.

"It's weird that we can't find anything out about her with all the government search engines our members can tap into," Soomie interjected. "The only reasons her information could possibly be that classified would be if (A) she's in witness protection, (B) she's the daughter of some international dignitary-slash-fugitive who's been given asylum by the government, or (C) she's got an assumed identity."

Ariana flinched and swallowed wrong, then started coughing uncontrollably. She covered her mouth with her hand and turned away, her heart racing.

"Are you all right?" Maria asked.

"I'm fine," Ariana croaked, coughing a few more times.

"Maybe we should talk to national about her," Maria suggested, sipping her espresso. A cool breeze tossed her wavy dark hair in front of her eyes, and she tucked it behind her ear. "I'm sure they have the resources to find Lily's family."

"We can't," Lexa said flatly. "They'll think we didn't properly vet our taps. Which, let's face it, we didn't. We just thought she was cool and liked her style and figured Headmaster Jansen wouldn't have let her into Privilege House if she wasn't worthy."

Lexa blushed slightly and cast an askance look at Ariana, as if she'd just said too much. Ariana's heart skipped a breath. Was Headmaster Jansen in Stone and Grave?

"And now we're screwed," Lexa continued. "She's already made it too far in the process. They'll think we've gotten sloppy, and I can't have that on my record."

Ariana eyed Lexa. Clearly this was something she was very concerned about—her image with national Stone and Grave. Apparently Lexa wasn't as effortlessly perfect as she'd been making herself out to be.

"Okay, then how about a private detective?" Maria asked, lifting her shoulders. "Maybe a professional would be able to figure out what we're missing."

Ariana's shoulder muscles curled. A PI? They wanted to hire a PI to look into Kaitlynn's past? A private investigator would follow her around. Take pictures. Maybe even run her image through some law-enforcement websites. A PI could easily find out that Kaitlynn wasn't who she said she was. That she was, in fact, a convicted murderer and fugitive. The former roommate of one Ariana Osgood.

"It's not a bad idea," Soomie put in, tugging a scone out of a wax paper bag. "That's what my dad does when he's hiring new execs. It's a routine part of the background check."

"A private investigator," Lexa mused, narrowing her eyes. "I like it. Why haven't we done this before?"

"Because we never needed to," Maria said. "Everyone else we've ever tapped has been from a prominent family. Like Ana," she said with a smile.

Ariana tried to smile back, but her organs were twisting together in new and seriously uncomfortable configurations. This couldn't happen. She simply could not let this happen.

"Maybe I'll look up a few investigators and set some meetings at my parents' house in town," Lexa said, sipping her latte.

"Why not just have them come here?" Soomie asked.

"And risk Lily seeing and asking questions? No way," Lexa said. "Besides, the administration might want to know what I was up to." She looked around at her friends. "Where would I find a reputable PI, do you think?"

"Not in the yellow pages," Maria said with a snort. She reached for her Coach bag and extracted her cell phone. "I'm sure my father has a guy in DC to recommend."

"Wait. Both of your dads use private investigators on a regular basis?" Lexa asked.

Soomie lifted one shoulder as she chewed. "We're talking about billion-dollar businesses, Lex," she said. "They don't mess around."

"Hi, Daddy," Maria said into her phone. "I just have a quick—

Yes. Yes, Daddy. I'm eating right now. No, Daddy. I'm not working out too hard. Well, how else do you expect me to get into a decent dance company unless I—" She listened for a few seconds, then groaned. "No, Daddy, I am not going to Harvard! We've been through this." She rolled her eyes at the girls and shoved herself up from the blanket, placing her hand over the phone. "This could take a while."

Maria gestured with her free hand as she paced away from the picnic blanket, sparring with her dad. Ariana's heart pounded with fear as she tried to figure out some way to discourage Lexa from her new plan. If she hired a PI and he uncovered Kaitlynn's true identity, it would all be over for both of them.

"I don't know about this, you guys," she said, her voice raspy thanks to her coughing fit and a seriously dry throat.

"Why not?" Lexa asked. "We need to know more about the girl before we can initiate her. We don't just let anyone in, you know."

"I know, but—"

"And in case it's not clear, this is all on the DL," Lexa told her. "Don't breathe a word of this to Lillian. Technically we shouldn't even be talking about this in front of a tap, but I thought you were going to help us out with some info on her."

Ariana slowly reached up and clutched her forearm, squeezing as hard as she could. Leave it to Lexa to find a way to put her back in her place as quickly as possible.

"Okay," Maria said, snapping her phone closed as she returned to the group. "My dad's going to set the meeting for eight o'clock on

Friday. The guy's name is Nathan Dove. I just texted his number to your phone," she told Lexa.

"Friday? But that's Halloween," Soomie pointed out. "What about the party?"

"My parents' house is ten minutes from yours," Lexa said. "I can pop out, meet this guy, and get back to the party before I'm even missed."

"Did you tell him what it's about?" Ariana asked Maria.

"Nah. My dad doesn't have time for minor details like why my friend might need to hire a detective," Maria joked, sitting again. "But he does have time for a rundown of my daily caloric intake and to badger me about my dream of being a dancer."

"He's just looking out for you," Soomie said, touching Maria's back.

Ariana's constricted lungs loosened slightly. At least the PI wouldn't know what Lexa wanted until they actually met. Which meant he wouldn't start looking into Kaitlynn until after his meeting with Lexa on Friday night. Ariana had until Friday to figure out a way to keep that meeting from happening.

She had until Friday to figure out how to stop Lexa Greene.

ALWAYS A WAY

Ariana sat in a comfy, cozy high-backed chair at the Hill on Wednesday night, feeling neither comfy nor cozy as she stared outside. The floor-to-ceiling windows were being pelted by heavy raindrops, the noise like a pair of rushing trains coming at her from both directions. In her hands was a latte, cold and untouched. Her eyes stung from being open and staring for so long, and when she blinked, her eyelids stuck for a moment before opening again.

There was no answer. No matter how many times she went over it in her head, she simply could not find a way out. Earlier today she had tried to talk Lexa out of meeting with the PI, saying it was a waste of time and money—not to mention a waste of a good party. That if the other Stone and Gravers hadn't found out anything about Lillian yet, then maybe that meant there wasn't anything to find out. But Lexa was unmovable. She even seemed excited. Apparently she was looking forward to playing a little cloak and dagger.

Little did Lexa know, however, that the moment this guy started to look into Lillian Oswald's past, a chain of events would be set in motion that would inevitably lead to Ariana landing back in prison. She had to stop Lexa. At whatever cost.

But every time Ariana thought about what that meant, she started to squirm. Yes, Lexa was putting Ariana's entire future at risk, but Lexa didn't know that. And technically, the girl hadn't done anything wrong. Yes, she'd been acting like a bitch lately, but she had a lot going on in her life, what with her parents' issues and all the publicity and the stress of having a history-free tap in Stone and Grave—plus the suspicion that one of her best friends was dating her ex. When Ariana thought about it diplomatically, the girl actually had a lot of reasons to be on edge. Besides, being bitchy, in and of itself, didn't warrant the ultimate punishment. If acting like a jerk meant getting offed, then half the population of this school would have been dead a long time ago.

Ariana groaned under her breath and placed her cup down on the carved oak table next to her chair. What was she going to do? How was she going to do it? And when?

"Anything I can do to help?"

Ariana looked up to find Jasper hovering over her with a cup of coffee and a chocolate croissant. The shoulders of his coat glistened with raindrops and his hair was completely soaked. She hadn't seen him come in or go to the counter, but then, she had turned her chair toward the window specifically so she wouldn't have to deal with anyone. She leaned back and sighed.

"No, thanks. I'm fine," she replied.

Jasper placed his food down next to Ariana's cup and sat on a footstool closer to the window to face her. "If you don't mind my saying so, you don't look fine."

Ariana fiddled with her fingers. "It's just . . . I don't know what I'm doing."

Jasper laughed and Ariana glowered at him. "It's not funny," she said curtly.

"Sorry." Jasper ran his hand over his mouth and straightened his face. "The very idea of you not knowing exactly what you're doing seems so implausible it made me laugh."

Ariana stared at him as he unbuttoned his coat and shrugged it off, getting up to hang it on a coatrack in the corner. He came back and sat in the same spot, resting his elbows on his knees.

"I don't understand," she said.

Jasper rubbed his hands together. "Ana, you radiate this intense level of self-assuredness that basically intimidates everyone around you," he said, his eyes sparkling. "Were you really not aware?"

A flattered blush crept across Ariana's face. "Well, I haven't felt very self-assured lately."

"Could have fooled me." Jasper reached underneath the footstool and inched it closer to her legs so that their knees were almost touching. "Tell me what the problem is. Maybe we can put our two evil minds together and figure out a way to fix it."

Ariana laughed. Yeah, right. Like she could really tell him what was going on.

"I can't," she said. "It's . . . private."

A dark cloud passed through Jasper's eyes, but it was gone even faster than it appeared. "Well, then, I'll just give you a general bit of wisdom and you can do with it what you will."

He reached out and took both Ariana's hands in his. Her instinct was to pull away, but then she looked into his eyes. They were so blue, so intense, so determined, she found herself frozen. His skin was insanely warm, odd considering he'd just come in from the storm of the century.

"Any situation . . . and I mean *any* situation . . . can be twisted to your advantage," he said, his voice low. "You are a creative, strong person, and you will find a way to not only fix the situation, but to benefit from it. The key, Ana, is to not give up. The key is to keep looking at this problem, whatever it is, from every angle you can possibly think of, until the answer presents itself."

Ariana stared into those hypnotic blue eyes, and just like that, her heart warmed, and she felt her uncertainty begin to melt away.

"The answer will just present itself," she said slowly.

"It will," he replied with utter confidence. He squeezed her hands, then released them and stood, gathering his food and drink. "Don't give up, Ana. That's the key. Never give up."

Then he grabbed his coat, folded it over his arm, and walked away. Ariana turned in her chair to watch him go. Then she sat back in her chair and smiled.

He was right, of course. There was always a way. How could she have forgotten that? Look how far she'd come already. Breaking out of prison, traveling across the country twice, faking her death, attending her own memorial service, creating a whole new life for herself, landing in all the honors classes she wanted at one of the most prestigious schools in the world, winning the heart of the most sought-after guy on campus.

There was always, *always* a way. Now all she had to do was find it.

THE PLAN

"Could someone hold my hair on so I can pin it?" Maria asked.

"Okay. That sounded weird," Kaitlynn said as she zipped up the skintight pants on her Catwoman costume.

"I've got it," Ariana offered, crossing Lexa and Maria's room to help Maria in front of the full-length mirror. Maria had chosen to dress up as Christine from *Phantom of the Opera*, and was adding tendrilled extensions to her hair to look more the part. She was wearing a big, frilly nightgown and a ton of heavy makeup.

"Wow, Ana. You look seriously freaky," Maria said with a grin, eyeing Ariana's reflection in the mirror.

"Thanks," Ariana replied. "I'm assuming that's a compliment."

"Oh, it is," Lexa said, sitting down on her bed to place her feet into her gold stiletto heels. "Where did you get that wig?"

Ariana glanced at Kaitlynn and smiled slightly as she touched the heavy gray and white wig that stood straight up from the top of her head. Her face was powdered white and she'd blackened the area around her eyes and bought a set of gross false teeth—though she wasn't wearing them yet. Her bride-of-Frankenstein dress was white and had gray gauzy layers. The bells of the wide sleeves fell almost to the ground.

She looked scary as hell. Palmer was going to love it.

"Lily and I got our costumes in town yesterday," Ariana said.

"What happened to dressing up together?" Lexa asked as she smoothed her blond Heidi Klum wig.

"I tried to get her to go superhero sexy with me, but she was all about the scare factor," Kaitlynn lied. Both of them had known exactly what costumes they were going to buy before they ever walked into the shop.

"Well, it works for you," Maria said, adding the last bobby pin to her hair. "That's it. Thanks, Ana." She turned around to face the room. "What do you guys think?"

"Totally Broadway worthy," Kaitlynn said.

"Well, I'm almost done," Lexa said. "I just need you guys to help me with the false lashes. I suck at those."

She grabbed a plastic box with two black caterpillar-like sets of lashes set against a piece of purple foam and headed for the bright lights of the bathroom. Kaitlynn and Maria moved to follow, but Ariana hung back, her heart skipping a beat as a perfect opportunity presented itself.

"I'll be right there," she said. "Just going to tweak the eye makeup."

Lexa shrugged and the three of them headed inside the bathroom. Checking over her shoulder, Ariana quickly grabbed Lexa's gold clutch and slipped her cell phone out of her bag. Her fingers trembling slightly, she scrolled through the contact list until she found private investigator Nathan Dove's number, then copied the number down on a Post-it. She had Lexa's cell back in her bag and the bag back on the desk where it had been before the girls returned from the bathroom.

One step down. Many, many more to go.

"Okay. It takes me an hour and many tears to get those things on, but Maria does it like it's putting on a Band-Aid," Lexa joked.

"Seventeen years, a couple dozen ballets. I've gone through thousands of those things," Maria said with a worldly smirk.

Lexa went straight for her purse. She pulled her phone right out and froze as she looked down at the screen. Ariana's heart all but stopped. Had she left Dove's number up on the screen? Could Lexa somehow tell she'd been messing with it?

"Soomie texted. She says everything's ready and to get our butts there ASAP," Lexa said with a laugh.

Ariana let out a sigh of relief.

"So. Are we all ready?" Lexa asked, tucking the phone inside the bag again. "Conrad's bringing the car around in about five minutes."

"Actually, I'm going to have to meet you guys there," Ariana said, glancing at her watch.

"What? Why? I thought we were all going over together," Maria said.

"She has a phone call with her grandmother," Kaitlynn explained, shrugging into her jacket, which looked kind of silly over her shiny nylon outfit.

"She wants an update on how things are going around here," Ariana lied. "I haven't been in touch in a while, so she's freaking out."

"You schedule calls with your grandmother?" Lexa asked flatly, looking up at Ariana through her fake blond bangs.

"You schedule calls with your parents," Ariana shot back.

"She makes a good point," Maria said to Lexa, picking up her white coat. "But doesn't old lady Covington realize it's Halloween?"

"She's in her eighties," Ariana replied. "She doesn't even know it's October."

The others laughed and finished gathering their things.

"But how will you get there?" Lexa asked, lifting the hair of her wig out from under the collar of her black coat.

"Don't worry about me. I'll just take a cab," Ariana said, walking them out and down the hall toward the elevators. She paused in front of the door to her room. "See you there."

The girls air-kissed her and waved as they made their way to the elevators. Ariana slipped into her room and closed the door behind her, her nerves jittery. She needed a few moments to herself to go over the plan. To make sure everything was in place. Her whole future, her very life, all hinged on tonight's events. Everything had to go perfectly.

Tugging her phone out of her bag, she entered in Dove's number and saved it into her contacts under "John Smith." Then she went to her desk and opened the top drawer. Sitting atop her pens and pencils was a long, brown envelope, inside of which was the compromising photo of Palmer. Ariana clenched her teeth as she stared down at it, then plucked it up and shoved it into her bag. She wasn't planning on using it—if all went well tonight, she wouldn't have to—but it was always good to be prepared.

Taking a deep breath, Ariana sat on the edge of her bed, closed her eyes, and took herself through the plan step by step by step, looking for any flaws—any potential hiccups. Finally satisfied, she opened her eyes again and looked around the room in satisfaction.

It was going to work. It had to. Her entire future depended on it.

HUSBAND AND WIFE

"Welcome to my haunted row house!" Soomie shouted, opening the door for Ariana. She had a huge smile on her face and some kind of black drink in one hand. Her eyes were unfocused, as if she'd already downed a few of those drinks, even though the party started just a half hour ago. Conversation and laughter gurgled out into the night air as Soomie grabbed Ariana's wrist and tugged her inside. "Where've you been?"

Ariana could smell the alcohol on her breath and tried not to scrunch her nose. Soomie was in a good mood for the first time in weeks. She didn't want to do anything to put a damper on it.

"I had to make a call." Ariana touched the skirt of her frayed dress. "What do you think?"

She struck a pose, tilting her head back so that her extremely tall and heavy gray and white wig almost took her down. She flashed her long black fake nails.

"Appropriately spooky," Soomie said. "What do you think of mine?"

Ariana looked Soomie up and down. She wore a light pink gown with delicate spaghetti straps, and a gorgeous, sparkling tiara. Her makeup was colorful and bright, and there were glittery stars pasted around her eyes.

"I like it. But I thought you were going goth," Ariana said.

Soomie sipped her drink and swallowed. "I changed my mind. This is my homage to Princess Brigit."

She reached down and tugged up the hem of the wide skirt. On her feet she wore a pair of pink sequined flats. The sight of them brought tears to Ariana's eyes. Brigit never wore heels—was never able to walk in them—until the night she died. The night that Kaitlynn and the rest of her friends convinced her it was time to try.

"That's really sweet, Soomie," Ariana said, her heart heavy.

"Don't look so sad," Soomie said, gripping Ariana's arm. "She's looking down on us right now and smiling. And besides, it's a party!"

She hooked her arm around Ariana's back and led her into the house. The place was small—thin and long, like any historical row house—but poshly decorated. The walls of the living room were painted a deep violet, and the fireplace was tiled in dark reds and ambers. Not that it was easy to take in the details. Soomie had gone all out with the Halloween decorations. Everything was covered with cobwebs, fake spiders, wispy ghosts, and leering monster masks. The bay window at the front of the house held ten expertly carved jack-o'-lanterns, each one more elaborately terrifying than the last.

"Okay, the first floor is for eating, drinking, conversation, and general merriment," Soomie said, sliding sideways to get through the crowd and dragging Ariana with her. "Upstairs, in the dining area, is the dance floor. I had the table and chairs moved to make room," she explained, pointing at the staircase. "On the third floor are the two bedrooms. You can imagine what they're being used for," she said. "But on the roof is the real fun."

"The real fun?" Ariana asked.

"Pumpkin carving, bobbing for apples, crap like that," Soomie said, waving her drink around.

"Really?" Ariana said, amused.

"Brigit lived for that stuff, so I figured, why not?" Soomie said. "And believe it or not, that's where almost everyone is. They *think* they're sophisticated and above it all, but they're so not."

Ariana laughed. "Okay. I'll go up and check it out."

"I'm right behind you," Soomie said. "I just have to check on the caterers."

"Okay. I'll see you up there," Ariana replied. "Oh, hey. Do you know where Lexa is?" she asked casually. "She hasn't left yet, has she?"

"No," Soomie said. "She's upstairs somewhere."

"Cool," Ariana said.

She made her way slowly up the slim staircase, pressing her back against the wall as a guy dressed as some Star Wars robot tromped down past her. On the second floor the music was pumping and strobe lights lit the dining room, affording flashing glimpses of goblins and ghouls and sports stars and superheroes. Kaitlynn was out there, moving to the music, but there was no sign of Lexa and Conrad. Ariana turned up the next flight of stairs and almost slammed into Marilyn Monroe making out with Shrek.

"Sorry," she said. But they didn't even come up for air. Both bedroom doors were closed, so Ariana quickly took the last flight of stairs and shoved open the door to the roof.

The night air was cool, but not biting. There were three long tables set up for pumpkin carving, and every seat seemed to be taken. Orange globe lights were strung from tall cornstalks all around the periphery of the roof, and overhead a huge full moon hung low over the city. Ariana walked around slowly, her heart pounding, looking out for Lexa, but also searching for her Frankenstein. As she came around to the back of the roof, behind the raised doorway, she spotted Palmer. He was standing with Rob, Christian, and Adam, cheering Landon on as he dove his face into a huge vat of apples and water. Even with a green face, a high forehead, and bolts sticking out of his neck, Palmer was the handsomest guy on the roof.

"Come on, Lan! You can do it!" Palmer shouted. "Where're your teeth, man?"

His friends cracked up laughing. Then Landon whipped his head up, his hair flicking back, spraying all of them in the face with a million droplets of water. They all shouted and raised their arms as Landon bit through the apple in his mouth and smiled.

"Told you I could do it," he said.

Ariana smiled. Her pulse racing, she wove slowly through the mingling crowd, waiting for Palmer to look up and spot her. She waited and waited, but he was too preoccupied with dotting the water from his face without messing up his makeup. Finally, Ariana was able to sneak up behind him and slip her hand into his.

"Hello, husband," she whispered in his ear.

Palmer turned around, took one look at her, and grinned. "You came."

"I did."

Then she stood up on her toes and kissed him. She kissed him until the other guys noticed and started shouting. Until they started clapping. Until they finally got bored and walked away.

"Wow," Palmer said, his eyelids heavy as he pulled away. "And in front of all these people. What if Lexa were here?"

Ariana smiled, looping her arm around her neck. "I'm no longer concerned about Lexa Greene," she said, her voice husky.

"Really?" he said. "What changed?"

"I remembered who I am," Ariana said.

Palmer's green brow knit. "Frankenstein's wife?"

Ariana laughed. "Exactly."

"Well then, *bride*," Palmer said. "Would you like to go downstairs and dance?"

Reluctantly, Ariana pulled away from him. "Maybe later. Right now I have something I need to take care of."

Palmer bit his lip. "Your task?" he whispered. "I heard you hadn't finished it yet."

Ariana's skin warmed. "Yeah. My task. But don't worry. It'll all be over by the end of the night. If I don't see you again here, I'll come by your room later, okay?"

"Works for me," Palmer replied with a grin. "Happy Halloween, my wife," he said, giving her a long, firm kiss.

Ariana couldn't have stopped smiling if she'd tried. "Happy Halloween, my husband."

MASTER MANIPULATOR

Ariana waited on the landing of the third floor, standing in the shadows, until she saw Palmer and his friends heading downstairs for some food. Then she quickly made her way up to the roof and toward the front of the house, where she would have a bird's eye view of the street below. As the party swelled and ebbed around her, Ariana patiently watched until she saw a girl in a blond wig and a black coat, carrying a gold clutch, rush out the front door and into a waiting cab. Her pulse raced in excitement.

Game on.

Quickly Ariana returned to the second floor. Kaitlynn was right where Ariana had last seen her, doing her own private dance in the center of the dance floor as if no one else was there, her eyes closed, her arms thrown over her head. Ariana watched her for a moment, letting Kaitlynn have her fun. But then, it was time. Time to put the final phase of the plan in motion. Time to end this, once and for all. Kaitlynn had a job to do, even though she didn't know it yet. A skitter of excitement raced over Ariana's skin but was quickly cooled by an icy cold shell of resolve. She took a deep breath, stormed through the room, and grabbed Kaitlynn's arm.

"Come on. We have to go," she said urgently.

"What? Go where?" Kaitlynn demanded, tripping in her cat-heels as she was dragged from the room.

"Anywhere," Ariana said under her breath as she reached the top of the stairs. She looked around behind her, checking over both her shoulders. "The jig is up, *Lily*. We're going on the run. Now."

Kaitlynn's eyes widened, an almost comical sight behind the black vinyl mask. "What? Why? What happened?"

Ariana huffed an impatient sigh and pulled Kaitlynn toward the far wall and the window overlooking the tiny, fenced-in backyard. She took in a shaky breath and looked Kaitlynn in the eye. "Lexa is hiring a private investigator to look into Lillian Oswald's past."

"What?" Kaitlynn stepped backward into the wall. "No. She wouldn't. She doesn't have the balls."

"Apparently she does," Ariana replied through her teeth. "And if he finds out the truth about you, he's going to find out the truth about me. We have to get out of here, Kaitlynn. We've had our fun, but it's over. We've gotta bail."

Ariana moved away, going for the stairs, but Kaitlynn's hand shot out and grabbed her arm. "Wait a minute."

"We don't *have* a minute," Ariana said impatiently.

"You said she's *hiring* a PI, not that she already hired him," Kaitlynn said, her eyes flat. "Has she met with him yet?"

Ariana blinked, confused. "No. Not yet. They're meeting tonight."

Kaitlynn's eyes narrowed. "Where?"

Ariana hesitated for a long moment. "What does it matter? Wait. You're not thinking of—"

"We have worked *way* too hard to get where we are," Kaitlynn said fiercely, stepping up to Ariana. "And I am not going to let that self-serving bitch ruin it. So tell me. Where the hell are they?"

"I . . . she said . . ." Ariana blinked a few times, tears of uncertainty shining in her eyes. "She said she was going to meet him at her parents' house to avoid suspicion."

"Address, please?" Kaitlynn said stoically.

Ariana fumbled with her purse and extracted her cell. She scrolled to Lexa's name and turned the screen to face Kaitlynn. Her eyes flicked to the address.

"Thanks, A," she said, shoving past Ariana. "I'll see you back at the room."

"Wait. Shouldn't we . . . I don't know . . . think about this?" Ariana said.

Kaitlynn paused at the top of the stairs, her hand clutching the filigree on the banister. She looked at Ariana and laughed derisively. "Being on the outside has softened you, A. Don't worry. I got this. You can thank me later."

Then she barreled down the stairs and was gone. Ariana turned shakily toward the window and looked down at the revelers below. Then she focused on her own reflection in the pane, took a deep breath, and lifted her lips in a smile as cold as ice.

FREED

Ariana had the cab drop her off five blocks from Lexa's parents' house. As the car pulled away, she yanked out her cell phone, dialed Nathan Dove, and started walking. He picked up on the third ring.

"Hello, Mr. Dove, this is Lexa Greene," Ariana said. "I'm so sorry, but I'm going to have to cancel our meeting."

"I was just on my way to meet you," the man replied, his voice gruff.

"I'm sorry for the late notice, but at least this way I won't take up any more of your time," Ariana said as she speed-walked along ivy-covered brick walls and past iron gates with serious security systems. She only hoped that Lexa's place didn't have such daunting barriers.

"Kids," Nathan Dove said. Then the line went dead.

Ariana shoved her phone back into her bag as she came around the corner and spotted the white-columned Greene manse across the street. She blew out a relieved sigh when she saw that the gates had, mercifully, been left open. Most likely Lexa had left them ajar for the private investigator.

As she scurried across the street, Ariana caught a disturbed look from an elderly couple walking their puggles. She almost shot them an annoyed glare in return until she remembered that she was dressed up as the Bride of Frankenstein. It might have been Halloween, but this wasn't exactly a big neighborhood for trick-or-treating. She ignored them, raced to the far sidewalk, and ducked through the gates in front of Lexa's house. The driveway was long and steep, and by the time Ariana made it to the front door she was out of breath. She narrowed her eyes to better see in the dark and saw that the door had been left yawning open. Kaitlynn was already here.

Steeling herself, Ariana ran for the door, imagining what must have occurred. Kaitlynn had probably decided to simply ring the front bell, knowing that Lexa would be surprised to see her, but would let her in. They were, after all, friends—even if Lexa was planning on having Lillian vetted by a detective. Then, the moment the door had swung open wide enough, Kaitlynn had attacked. The element of surprise was always quite helpful in situations such as these, a fact that both Ariana and Kaitlynn knew well.

Sure enough, as soon as Ariana's foot hit the front step, she heard a crash. She ducked through the door, her heart in her throat, and followed the noise to the parlor just off the foyer. She froze when she saw Kaitlynn and Lexa locked in a struggle. Lexa's blond Heidi Klum wig was strewn on the floor, and she'd lost one stiletto heel as Kaitlynn dragged her backward, her fingers clenched around her throat. Ariana ducked behind a tremendous planter. She watched as Lexa's thin fingers clawed at Kaitlynn's white-knuckled hands. Watched as Kaitlynn clenched her jaw and pressed her lips together, her eyes narrowed and nostrils flared from the effort. Watched as Lexa's legs began to twitch. As her life began to leave her.

It was fascinating, watching it all from the outside. Playing the part of spectator.

Lexa's eyes started to roll into the back of her head, and Ariana took her cue. She plucked a large blue-and-white china vase from a table, walked up behind Kaitlynn, and smashed the vase into the back of her head, right near the base of her skull. Kaitlynn slumped forward, releasing her grip on Lexa, who fell to the floor choking and coughing and writhing around, her miniskirt riding so far upward that her black panties were exposed.

Ariana stood over Kaitlynn for a moment, her chest heaving up and down. This was going to feel so, so good. It was all she could do to keep from smiling. She had to be careful, though. Lexa might see.

Kaitlynn turned over with a groan and blinked a few times, clearly dazed. But when her eyes fell on Ariana, it was like everything snapped into focus. She shoved herself to her feet, her teeth clenched, and let out an inhuman shriek, vaulting herself at Ariana.

This time, however, Ariana was the one who was ready for the assault. As Lexa crawled across the room, her back to Ariana, Ariana grabbed the charging Kaitlynn by the shoulders, turned to the side, and used Kaitlynn's own momentum to fling her through the nearest window. The crash was satisfying, the blood even more so. Kaitlynn lay crooked forward over the windowsill, scratches all over her arms, a gash through the black vinyl around her stomach. Ariana plucked a particularly sharp shard of glass from the window frame and hovered over Kaitlynn as she struggled to turn over, coughing up blood and spittle.

"You said . . . you said we were friends," she whispered to Ariana, convulsing.

"I say a lot of things," Ariana whispered to her. She lifted the shard of glass and let Kaitlynn get a nice, long look at it. "This is for Brigit," she whispered.

Kaitlynn's green eyes widened just before Ariana slashed her across the throat. She twitched twice, big full-body twitches as her lifeblood seeped out all over the bushes just outside the window frame. And then, with one last gurgling cough, she closed her eyes, and it was over.

It was finally, finally over.

Ariana lifted Kaitlynn's hand, slid the purple bangle from her wrist, and shoved it on over her own hand, adding it to the red one she already wore. She could practically hear Brigit's laugh of triumph in her ears.

"Ana!" Lexa ran up behind Ariana and barreled into the back of her shoulder, clinging to her as she looked down at Kaitlynn's broken, bloody corpse. "Omigod, Ana. What did you do?" she choked out.

Ariana dropped the shard of glass with which she had just freed herself and turned to Lexa, shaking. "I just saved your life."

"We have to call the police," Lexa said, turning away from the body, tears streaming down her face. The fake eyelashes were peeling free and her black eyeliner was smudged all the way to her cheekbone. Her hand went to her throat, where Ariana could see a series of angry red bruises left behind by Kaitlynn's fingers.

"Wait!" Ariana blurted, sounding panicked, even to her own ears. Lexa froze and Ariana wrung her hands on the skirt of her costume for effect. The white fabric was already splattered with red dots, and the blood on her hands made it much worse. Such a shame. She was going to have to burn her outfit and lose the deposit. Although, for now, the blood did lend a certain added touch of Halloween spookiness to the ensemble. "Just wait. We have to think."

"Think? About what?" Lexa said, groping in her purse for her phone. She was shaking all over and gasping for breath. "Ana, Lillian's dead!"

It was all Ariana could do to keep from grinning at the words. *Lillian's dead. Dead, dead, dead.* The word danced a happy jig in her head. She took a deep breath and reminded herself she was supposed to be freaking out.

"I know. I know, okay? I just . . . let's just take a second and calm down." Ariana crossed over to Lexa, biting down on her own tongue to bring tears into her eyes. She sat down on the brocade couch, tugging Lexa with her, making sure to keep the bloody bit of her dress folded toward her lap.

"Calm down? Are you serious? Lily just tried to choke me to death and now she's over there . . . she's over there. . . ." She looked at the window, horrified, then looked away, covering her mouth with her quaking hand. "We have to call the police. We have to!"

"Omigod," Ariana said, crossing her arms over her stomach and leaning forward, as if the realization of what she'd done had just hit her. She and Lexa had to be in this together. Lexa could never suspect the truth of tonight's events. "Omigod, omigod, omigod."

"Okay. It's going to be okay," Lexa rambled. "Ana, take a breath. If you lose it, I'm gonna lose it, and we can't both lose it right now."

Ariana breathed in deeply through her nose, letting Lexa comfort her.

"But you're right," she said tremulously, looking over at the body as if horrified. "Lillian's dead. And I—"

"You saved my life," Lexa said, with the faintest hint of clear-headedness.

Exactly, Ariana thought. *Let's let that fact sink in now, shall we?*

Her plan was working like a charm. By setting Kaitlynn up to try to kill Lexa, then swooping in at the last minute to play the hero, Ariana had earned Lexa's trust. Her gratitude. Her undying devotion. Plus one big, fat future favor.

Lexa just hadn't realized any of this yet. But she would. Jasper had been right. She had not only found a way to fix the situation, she had found a way to twist it in her favor. The only person on Earth who knew Ariana's true identity was dead. And Lexa—the one person who could make or break her future—was forever in her debt.

Ariana was too proud of herself for words.

"She was going to kill me, Ana," Lexa said. "But you . . . you stopped her."

For a long moment, Lexa and Ariana looked into each other's

eyes, and Ariana knew that Lexa understood. The two of them were bonded for life. And Lexa no longer had the power to hold anything over Ariana's head ever again.

"The police will understand," Lexa said, reaching into her bag for their phone. "You were just trying to help me."

"But what if they don't?" Ariana said, her bottom lip trembling as she shoved herself up from the couch. Lexa's brows came together and Ariana looked around the room wildly, as if confused—terrified. "What if they think . . . what if they think we murdered her?"

"What? Why would they think that?" Lexa said, getting up as well. She fiddled with her cell phone with both hands.

"Think about it, Lex," Ariana said desperately, throwing her hands out. "You were hiring a PI to look into Lillian's past. It's going to look like you had something against her."

Lexa whirled around to face the door, one hand flying to her mouth. "Omigod. Dove! He's on his way here right now!"

She hit a speed dial button on her cell phone. Ariana knew what Lexa was about to do, and that it was pointless, but she let her do it anyway.

"Hi, Mr. Dove? It's Lexa Greene. I'm sorry, but I'm not going to be able to make our meeting," Lexa said into the phone.

Then she flinched and hit the off button.

"What'd he say?" Ariana asked.

"He said 'I know that, schizo,' and hung up," Lexa replied, looking baffled but relieved.

Ariana bit her tongue to keep from laughing. It was now time to deal the final blow. To get this thing moving so they could both get on with their lives.

"Wait. What about your parents?" she said, her eyes wide. "They're not—"

"Omigod. My parents." Lexa pressed the heels of her hands against her eyes. "My father . . . this would destroy his career," she said, dropping her arms again. "An attempt on my life? A murderer in his house? He's already been dragged through the mud the past few weeks, but this . . . he'd never recover. And he'd kill me."

Ariana stepped forward and slipped the cell phone from Lexa's fingers. She turned it off and tossed it on the couch. "Then we definitely cannot call the police," Ariana told her, squeezing her hand. "You make that call and within ten minutes this place will be crawling with detectives and dogs and CSI guys. Not to mention about a hundred reporters, a news helicopter, and a million paparazzi."

"You're right," Lexa said, nodding. "We have to make this go away."

Spoken like a good politician's daughter, Ariana thought wryly.

Lexa stared at the body, the legs dangling against the wall, the head and arms trailing into the backyard.

"What about her family?" Lexa said slowly.

"As far as we know she doesn't even have any," Ariana reminded Lexa.

"But what if she does? What if they come looking for her?" Lexa asked tremulously.

"Then we just tell them Lillian up and left one morning. No note, no anything. And we have no idea where she went."

"Do you think that will work?" Lexa asked, looking into Ariana's eyes. Looking for assurances. Some way to assuage her fear and guilt. Ariana stared back, trying to be the picture of certainty she knew her friend needed.

"I haven't seen her call a soul since she's been here. She never mentioned brothers or sisters or parents," Ariana said in a firm tone. "Maybe Soomie was right. Maybe she was a poseur. Maybe she stole her identity. But trust me, whatever the case may be, Lillian Oswald does not exist." She took both Lexa's hands now, her friend's fingers cold inside her warm grip. "Don't let a ghost ruin your life. Not to mention your father's career."

Lexa nodded slowly, then sniffled. "You're right. Okay. What do we do?"

"We need to find somewhere to bury the body."

Lexa turned and paced away from Ariana, away from the horror of Kaitlynn's corpse, bringing her fingers to her mouth as she thought.

"The pet cemetery," she said, whirling around. "It's in the very back of the yard. My mom never goes back there because it makes her too sad. If we put her under the rosebushes back there, no one will notice."

Ariana nodded. "Let's get to work."

COVER-UP

"You'll take care of it?" Lexa said to Keiko Ogaswara, handing her a wad of cash.

"Of course, Lex. That's what I'm here for," Keiko replied. "But are you sure you're all right?"

Lexa and Ariana had decided they would tell Keiko that they had brought a couple of boys from school back to the house and that Lexa had gotten into an argument with one of them. Being slightly drunk, she'd grabbed the blue-and-white vase and thrown it at him, but he'd ducked and the vase had gone through the window. Lexa had hurled the vase out for good measure, cringing as the piece—worth thousands of dollars—clipped the pane and shattered.

"I'm fine. Really. Just embarrassed. You won't tell my father, right?" Lexa said. "You know how he feels about reckless behavior."

"Of course I won't tell him," Keiko said, shaking her head and ducking her chin. "Have I ever let slip any of your indiscretions in the past?"

Ariana raised one eyebrow and eyed Lexa. What indiscretions was Keiko talking about?

"No. It's just . . . this is really important," Lexa said, glancing past Keiko at the broken window. She and Ariana had meticulously cleaned the blood away before phoning Keiko, but the pane was still shattered. "I didn't even tell them I was going to be here tonight."

"You have nothing to worry about," Keiko said, touching Lexa's arm. "Now you two should go. It's Halloween and you're all dressed up." She smirked down at the skirt of Ariana's costume. "Like the fake blood, by the way. Very realistic."

Lexa turned green so fast Ariana was sure she was going to faint. She placed her hand on the small of her friend's back. "Thanks."

"You should go out and have some fun," Keiko said.

Ariana and Lexa exchanged a tired, amused, resigned look. "Right. Fun," Lexa said. "That's what this night is supposed to be for."

She turned and grabbed her purse, opening the door so that Ariana could walk out first. "Thanks again, Keiko!" As soon as the heavy door closed behind them, Ariana let out a breath.

"Do you think she bought it?" Ariana asked.

"It doesn't really matter," Lexa said. "She's not going to tell anyone. She knows that staying on my good side means staying on my dad's good side."

Ariana nodded, feeling secure in the steps they had taken to cover up Kaitlynn's death. The rose bushes out back still had their leaves and even some of their flowers, and after burying Kaitlynn good and deep, then replacing all the earth, their branches completely covered the evidence. They'd worn gloves, and Lexa had made sure to place all the tools back in the workmen's shed, just as they'd found them—slightly dirty, but not too dirty. Kaitlynn was dead and buried. Really and truly gone. And Ariana was really and truly free.

"We should go somewhere and make sure people see us," Ariana said. "Like for an alibi."

"An alibi?" Lexa said, paling all over again.

"I'm sure we won't need one," Ariana assured her. "But just in case."

Lexa looked around at the peaceful front yard, the lights glowing alongside the driveway, the holly bushes lining the walk.

"Well . . . I know a bar. . . ."

"Perfect," Ariana said, slipping her arm around Lexa's companionably. Lexa gave her an odd look, but Ariana chose to ignore it. She whipped out her phone to call a cab. "Let's go."

FRIENDSHIP

The bar in Georgetown was packed with an odd mix of Washington interns just off work, their collars loosened, their jackets flung over the backs of green vinyl booths, and college-aged Halloween revelers, dressed up as everything from Playboy bunnies to Supreme Court justices. The walls were paneled with dark wood and lined with bookshelves stuffed with old and important-looking tomes, and the bartenders all wore suits, topped by masks of their favorite politicians.

"This is perfect," Ariana said, yelling to be heard over the shouting and laughing.

"For what? An after-murder drink?" Lexa whispered back sarcastically. She'd put her Heidi Klum wig on again, and her pink sequined dress looked none the worse for the attempt on her life. If not for the dark circles under her eyes and the slightly smudged makeup, no one would have known anything was amiss.

"Okay. That's the last time we utter the *M* word," Ariana said, her eyes cutting. "This is not something we can casually talk about. And remember—it was self-defense."

"I know," Lexa said, turning sideways to try to find a path through the jammed-in bodies. "You're just going to have to give me a few days to get used to it."

"Hey! My woman's here!" a guy in a Frankenstein mask shouted, trying to loop his arm around Ariana's waist.

"Sorry," she said, shoving his hands away. "This bride is spoken for."

She pushed her way to the bar and ordered two dry martinis from Bill Clinton. No one had checked their IDs at the door. Which, possibly, was the reason Lexa knew of this place and liked it.

"You seem so chill," she said to Ariana.

"It's called acting," Ariana lied. She reached past Lexa and took her drink, which Bill was holding out for her. "It's going to take at least ten of these to calm my nerves."

She glanced around as Lexa paid for their drinks, and saw a couple dressed up as Sleeping Beauty and her prince getting up from two stools nearby.

"Seats!" she shouted, sliding in to claim them.

A pair of overgrown babies in diapers and footie-pajamas had been gunning for the stools, but Ariana slapped her hand down on the second, saving it for Lexa, who was still struggling through the crowd.

"Sorry. This one's mine," she told them.

The babies grumbled something under their breath and walked away. Lexa appeared, sank onto the stool, and slumped her shoulders, resting her drink on the bar. She took a deep breath and looked at Ariana out of the corner of her eye before straightening her posture.

"So." Lexa gave her a long and serious look. "I suppose you can now consider your S and G task complete."

Ariana sipped her drink to cover her grin, then sat up straight, the heavy wig of her bride of Frankenstein costume threatening to pull her backward. "I did complete it, though. I just . . . hadn't turned it in yet."

"Did you?" Lexa said, lowering her glass from her lips. "You really compromised your precious relationship with the ex-love of my life?"

Ariana's jaw dropped slightly, surprised that Lexa had caved and been the first to mention it.

"I've known about you and Palmer since the night of the NoBash," Lexa said, placing the glass on an orange and black cocktail napkin. "For two people trying to keep their fling a secret, you really couldn't have been more obvious."

Ariana swallowed hard. The insult stung, but she didn't want to show it.

"Well, I knew all along that you were president of Stone and Grave," she lied. "For someone trying to keep her position of power secret, you really couldn't have been more obvious."

Lexa's lips twisted into a wry smile. She and Ariana looked at each other for a long moment, and Ariana could see the respect building in Lexa's eyes. Finally, Lexa lifted her glass and tilted it toward Ariana's. Their rims clicked and they both took nice, long drinks.

"So. A truce, then?" Lexa suggested, placing her glass down and laying her hands flat on the leather edge of the bar.

"Palmer and I don't have to hide anymore?" Ariana asked.

"And I will stop being such a raving bitch," Lexa said with a nod.

Ariana smiled as Lexa turned her stool and shifted her knees toward Ariana. "We're going to have to have each other's back now," she said seriously. "After everything that's happened tonight, everything we've done . . . the pettiness just seems so . . . petty."

Ariana nodded her agreement. "You're right." She looked into Lexa's eyes. "I've really missed my friend, Lex."

Lexa sighed. "I know. I've missed you too, Ana."

Then she reached forward and threw her arms around Ariana's neck. Ariana squeezed Lexa back.

"Okay. I'd better go," Lexa said, checking her delicate gold watch. She took a final swig of her drink, then plucked one of the olives from its skewer with her teeth. "I have official S and G business to take care of, and now's not the time to start shirking duties."

Ariana raised an eyebrow with interest. "Anything I can help with?"

Lexa gave her a wry smirk. "Not yet. You may have saved my life, but you *are* still a tap."

"God, please don't let it be any more hazing," Ariana joked.

"You'll see!" Lexa said, sliding off her stool.

Ariana was impressed. An hour ago Lexa had been shaking in her stilettos, but she seemed to be bouncing back quickly. Maybe she really was her father's daughter. Maybe she'd realized that there was no use dwelling on Kaitlynn's death. That the past was in the past.

Lexa grabbed her purse, paused in front of Ariana, and gave her one last hug. "Talk to you later?"

"Yeah," Ariana said.

She watched Lexa as she wove her way through the boisterous crowd. They shared a huge secret now, and she was impressed with how well Lexa was handling it. But then, she supposed one didn't get to be president of a hallowed secret society like Stone and Grave without possessing some serious strength of character.

With a content sigh, Ariana turned toward the bar again. She picked up her martini glass and looked at her odd, white-faced, black-eyed reflection in the mirror behind the bar. For the first time all night, she allowed herself one big, genuine smile. As a girl in a flapper costume claimed Lexa's empty seat, Ariana lifted her glass to herself in a toast.

Here's to your future, Briana Leigh Covington.

She brought the rim of the glass to her lips, and a dainty, red-fingernailed hand fell on her arm. The alcohol splashed over the edge onto Ariana's lap.

"Omigod! It can't be. . . . *Ariana?*"

Ariana's heart turned to stone inside her chest. She knew that voice better than she knew her own. Slowly, she lowered her glass. Her pulse pounded so hard she felt all the blood rush out of her head and into her fingertips and toes. When she turned to the right, she found herself looking directly into the wide brown eyes of Kiran Hayes.

"Holy crap! It *is* you!" Kiran threw her skinny arms around Ariana's neck and practically fell into her, clearly drunk off her ass. "Dude!

What're you doing here?" she wailed. "I thought you were supposed to be, like, dead!"

A couple of guys turned to look and Ariana bit her lip hard, then smiled at them, rolling her eyes. "She's totally wasted."

The guys laughed and turned away. She gripped Kiran's shoulders and pushed her back so that they were facing each other once again, then forced her features into an excited smile.

"Omigod, Kiran! I have *so* much to tell you!"

Then she hugged her old friend again and closed her eyes. This one was going to hurt.

CLARITY

"Omigod, if you buy me one more drink I'm not even gonna be able to walk out of here," Kiran said, leaning the full weight of her body into Ariana's shoulder. Her heeled shoes dangled from her fingers and her eyes were at half-mast. "No more alcohol for Kiran!"

"Wow. I don't remember the last time I heard you say 'when,'" Ariana teased with a laugh, swallowing back a lump of something that felt a hell of a lot like guilt.

"I know, right?!" Kiran blurted, her breath so rank Ariana almost fainted. "I'm so not that self-control girl. Unlike you!" She shoved Ariana hard, but Ariana didn't move. Instead Kiran was the one who almost fell over.

"Okay. I see your point," Ariana said, struggling to hold her limp friend up. Luckily she only weighed about ninety pounds. "I guess we should go."

Kiran smiled and flung one arm over Ariana's shoulders. "I'm so glad you talked me out of going to that Ford party," she said, rolling her hand around as they struggled for the door. Even in her inebriated state, Kiran caught the appreciative leers of more than one hot guy along the way. "It was gonna be all fat politicians trying to grope me anyway. Soooo pointless."

"Seriously," Ariana said, nodding her thanks to the ninja who held the door for them. "I don't know how you do it."

"I don't know how *you* do it!" Kiran said with a laugh. "I mean, faking your own death? That's so cool. Do you know that I was at your memorial service? I totally was. And everyone was crying and stuff. It was intense! You should've been there."

Ariana smirked.

"It must be so weird, though . . . like, not being able to talk to your old friends. But you can talk to me now!" She attempted to stand up straight and tripped, bracing herself against a lamppost. "I wanna say something."

Ariana took a deep breath and counted to ten as a group of college kids checked out Kiran, laughing at her serious wastedness. Every person that noticed the two of them was a potential threat.

"What do you want to say?" Ariana asked, hooking her arm around Kiran's waist and hurrying her across the street.

"I wanna say that I'm *glad* you got rid of Thomas Pearson," Kiran said, gesturing with her clutch purse. "I mean . . . honestly? I *never* liked that guy. What a total jackass."

Ariana forced a laugh as she and Kiran hit the sidewalk on the far side of the street. Luckily, there wasn't a ton of traffic. It was getting late, and most people had either turned in for the night or were still out celebrating at their Halloween parties. She cut left to walk along Key Bridge, knowing that she was going to have to get this over with as quickly as possible. If a police cruiser came by, not only would her hastily constructed plan be foiled, but she and Kiran would probably end up being hauled off for drunken disorderly behavior. Resolved, Ariana ducked her head and clung to Kiran's side as if she'd never let her go.

Ariana's throat closed up and tears prickled at her eyes.

Don't do this, she told herself. *Don't get emotional. She doesn't care about you. She never came to visit you at the Brenda T. She never even called. The girl is a drunken waste of space who will probably end up dead of an overdose soon anyway. Really, you're doing her and the little girls of the world a favor. One less wacked-out supermodel to look up to.*

Or maybe . . . maybe she could just let it go. Kiran was completely gone anyway. There was a solid chance that she would wake up tomorrow and not remember anything that happened tonight. Or, at the very least, assume she imagined it. Maybe she didn't have to do this.

"Omigod! You know what we should do? We should call Noelle!" Kiran said, stopping suddenly at the center of the bridge as a Porsche zipped by them, its engine revving. She whipped out her cell phone with surprising dexterity, then tripped sideways toward the guardrail. The light atop the nearest lamppost dimmed suddenly, and it was like a sign. A wake-up call. Just like that. Ariana no longer felt nostalgic or sorry or hesitant.

"Wait . . . what speed dial is she . . . ?" Kiran said, fiddling with the phone.

Ariana looked both ways. There were no cars coming. She had to do this. She had to do it now.

"K, I'm really sorry about this," Ariana said coolly.

"What?" Kiran looked at her, her brown eyes unfocused.

Then, Noelle's voice crackled through the phone, just loud enough for Ariana to hear, and all the air whooshed out of her lungs. Kiran held up one finger to Ariana, as if to say, "Hold that thought."

"Kiran! Nice to not call me back, bitch!" Noelle exclaimed. "I have *so* much to tell you!"

Ariana practically salivated. Noelle. Noelle was right there. Right on the other end of the line.

"Omigod, me first," Kiran said into the phone. "You're never going to believe—"

And just like that, Ariana's mind went blank. She placed both hands on Kiran's shoulders and shoved her over the side of the bridge. Kiran's mouth dropped into an O, her cell phone hit the ground, and then she was gone. She never even made a sound as she plummeted into the frigid dark water of the Potomac.

Ariana glanced quickly over the side to make sure she didn't surface, even though she was certain she wouldn't. Kiran had never been the best swimmer, and she had enough alcohol in her size-zero body to fell a professional wrestler. Satisfied that she was safe, Ariana clutched the bell sleeve of her dress and used it to pluck the damaged phone off the asphalt so as not to leave fingerprints.

"Believe what?" Noelle was saying. "Kiran? Hell-*o*? Are you there?"

Her mouth dry, Ariana held the phone to her ear.

"Kiran? Kiran?" Noelle said. "I can hear you breathing."

Ten million emotions rushed through Ariana's chest and into her throat, choking her off with a sob. Noelle. She was hearing Noelle's voice for the first time in years. It was all she could do not to laugh, not to cry, not to shout a million epithets at the girl who had played a role in so many of her perfect memories, and then taken away her entire life with one backstabbing move.

"*Kir*-an!" Noelle sang. "You have five seconds to sober up and speak before I hang up. Five . . . four . . . three . . . two—"

Ariana pressed her covered thumb into the END button. Then she took her first breath in a good two minutes and tossed the phone over the side of the bridge. With that, Ariana quickly started to walk, not wanting to be spotted lingering at the scene of her latest crime any longer than she had to.

As she reached the far side of the bridge, Ariana took one long, deep breath, and a single tear slid down her cheek, cutting a river in her stark white makeup. Then she rolled her shoulders back, lifted her head, and walked away.

Ally Ryan is about to discover that it turns out you can go home again, but it will pretty much suck.

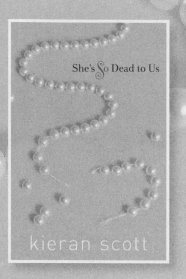

She's So Dead to Us

kieran scott

The first book in a new series about losing it all and being better off, from author Kieran Scott.